RAZE VS SNATCHERS

Raze vs Snatchers

Book one in the Raze Warfare series

SHELLEY CASS

For those who are a work in progress.
For those who are willing to be Raze in their own way.
For those who know that love is love, and how greatly the world needs it.

RECEIVE YOUR EXTRA RAZE WARFARE CHAPTER WHEN YOU SIGN UP FOR SHELLEY CASS' VIP LIST. GET YOUR BONUS HERE:

shelleycass.com/coming-soon-02

Razes, Razes everywhere.
Snatchers, Snatchers all beware…

| 1 |

One

"I'm fine," Kiddo stated. "I'll get it done." He slouched in his chair, his leg bouncing up and down rapidly. "Yes. Definitely fine."

Kid silenced his phone and lightly tossed it onto a pile of open books, picking up a pen to fidget.

"Hato doesn't normally seem the type to check up on people," a curious voice mused, and Kid stiffened.

"Sorry," Kiddo muttered. "Thought I was alone." He glanced over his shoulder with a slight frown.

He should have been alone. This was a private library. It was night. And he did not recognise the stranger, seated comfortably in the large arched window's sill.

"Oh, I'm not shushing you," the stranger quirked a smile. His sharp featured face was half in shadow from the dimness of the library, and half illuminated by the moonlight outside.

The moon's face was so full, it seemed it was nearly pressed to the window pane, as if it wanted to hug the stranger.

"Are you really fine, or did you want Hato to think you

were?" the stranger asked, shifting a little where his back leaned against the large frame.

His long legs were stretched out across the wide sill, as if it had been made to be this person's own rest stop, though Kid had never given the sill a second glance.

The stranger looked like he was framed in a photograph.

Kiddo blinked, still frowning. "Are you new?"

"I've been around here a few times before, but I'm new to you," the stranger answered, tilting his head to regard Kid.

Kid didn't recognise this young man as a friend of anyone else's in the gang, but Hato collected people from all over, even if not all of them came to live in the fold.

Nobody got in without being welcomed or forced to be in. So Kid shrugged, turning back to his books.

He twitched his pen between his fingers, trying to focus, but feeling the stranger's eyes on his back. He could feel his leg jiggling and tried to stop it.

"So, Hato doesn't normally check in on people," the stranger repeated with interest. "What's not fine about you?"

Kiddo rubbed at his face, messing the thick hair that swept over his brow.

"I'm fine," Kid answered again.

"Definitely. From what I can see." The young man waited expectantly for greater elaboration.

Kid sighed. "He's making sure I get my homework done."

The stranger gave a startled chuckle. "Hato? Checking you're doing your homework?"

"And then the bookwork. It's a school night."

"You're up late for a school night," the stranger commented.

"And that's what Hato said," Kid remarked dryly, clicking his pen. "I don't sleep much."

"Teenagers love to sleep," the stranger grinned. "Don't they?"

Kid pulled a face, hunching lower in his seat. This person had to be just a year or two older than himself. Eighteen or so.

"You're the one they call Kiddo, is that right?" the young man asked. He arched his spine like a slow, luxurious cat, getting the kinks out, before sliding down from the sill. He crossed to the large table covered in Kid's books, and sat against it so that they could talk more easily, without only seeing angles of each other.

Kiddo gave a nod, but watched the stranger warily, aware that this was in fact the most he had talked to anybody in as long as he could remember.

As the 'kid' brother adopted by the group, he rarely had a voice to contribute when planning or revelling was taking place. He didn't take part in the same things that the rest of the gang did. And he preferred to lone it at school.

"Is that why the boss man is checking up on you?" the stranger asked. "They baby you. And put you through school – to make you a better life than theirs?"

Hato had paid generously for all of them to up-skill or complete courses if they'd wanted to. Each member had come with some valuable contribution they could make to the group – like Jingle, and her incredible tech skills. But as Kiddo was the only one still sticking with high school, Hato definitely watched him closely, and with high hopes.

Kid consciously stilled his jumping leg. "I'm a sloppy student. But they're not a bunch of disappointed mums."

It was odd to think of the other gang members, all tough as nails, as babying anyone. But he supposed they did.

"They would be disappoint*ing* mums, all down there in the underground club, letting off steam with their youngen up here alone," the stranger remarked. "But you can't be too bad with classes if Hato trusts you with the books to his enterprise. You must be quite brilliant."

Kid was fidgeting again. He scowled and stopped himself. "I have a head for numbers and a way with words, when they come to me. But I do not have the ability to concentrate or sit still."

"You don't mind being left up here while they party down there?"

"It's their business. Up to them how they run it." If this person didn't know what the gang were up to, Kiddo didn't feel the need to get into it.

The stranger crossed his arms, the moonlight making his black leather jacket glint with silver. "They seem to get the fun side of things."

"I don't find fights and liquor to be that fun."

The stranger leaned closer. "And the other side of the business?"

"Like I said. I don't find fights to be that fun."

With a slow nod, the stranger pressed a finger to Kid's chest. There was a small lotus flower tattooed on the side of that finger, unfurling.

"I can see why they collected you. Why Hato keeps you safe."

Then the stranger straightened suddenly, and headed through the aisles of bookshelves towards the doors. "I'll let you focus, so you don't stay up too long into what's left of the night."

Kiddo blinked after the stranger, non-plussed to find himself so quickly alone and enfolded in quiet once more.

His leg was jumping again, and despite the young man's words he had no idea himself why the gang kept him around – aside from charity. He spent most of his time keeping out of the way. All he could do to try to make up for being a chaotic mess all the time was to do his best to run things behind the scenes for them.

Kid tried to ignore the stranger's musings, and tried instead to take his advice – to focus.

As usual, concentration was an elusive state he could not quite achieve. It wasn't that he was slow. But his head worked too fast. Sensations, ideas, thoughts, numbers, words, letters all came at him too quickly and sharply, and he had to consciously rein them in one at a time to address them. Pulling them all together until they made sense as a bigger picture rather than just whirling by like throwing stars.

When he had finally wrangled together the streams of numbers, and the letters into words into paragraphs and pages for an inventory report, he had half forgotten the stranger, and managed to pass out on the library couch for the hour or so before his alarm was set to go off.

| 2 |

Two

"I'll man The Lair tonight," Quicklips announced, pushing his plate toward the stack that Kid was piling up.

Quicklips had either got a smudge of sauce on his muscle top, or somebody's red lipstick had rubbed on the white material. Kid rolled his eyes, dumping the plates by the sink and then gesturing for the singlet.

"Flip's back in town. He'll be working with us tonight, so he and Seethe can be your brawn," Hato agreed, nodding slowly.

Quicklips grinned unashamedly and dragged the singlet over his head to hand to Kiddo. It was lipstick. A much harder stain to get out.

Kid had blotted and tossed the singlet in with the other whites, and pulled the door to the laundry room closed again in time to hear Velvet speaking.

"Underage night is our best chance to pick up any scouts checking out the young talent," Velvet drawled. "We need someone truly ripe for the picking to be the bait." Her dark eyes cut to Kid. "Young, fresh meat."

Kid glowered at her, and snatched her plate as he passed, headed back to the sink.

"He *is* really growing into his looks," Seethe tipped back his beer, boots up on the table, leaving dirty marks. "All youthful abs and metabolism."

Kid plonked the dishes into the soapy water, glaring at the pair of them.

Velvet was like a Somali queen, while Seethe was an ash blonde block of ice.

Kid had a strange kind of total trust and complete dislike for Velvet and Seethe. Velvet because she was sly, and Seethe because he hated everyone and everything. Except when it came to gang loyalty. They were both totally committed.

Not that that would keep them from offering Kid up as a sacrifice to whatever their cause was.

"Tiny, Jingle and Trix have bait duty covered," Hato glowered. "They can still look like ditched kids, and pack a punch."

"You betcha," Trix snickered. She lovingly ran electric blue nails over her new knuckle duster. Her fringe of afro curls was tied up sweetly by a pink scrunchy, revealing an edgy undercut. The ensemble was completed by a geisha style pin poked through her do, which Kiddo knew was actually a rather lethal skewer blade.

The always grouchy, but inarguably innocent looking Tiny blew a smoke ring up over their heads. "I'll wear a cute jumper," he rumbled.

He would need to hide his brawn to seem younger, or his short stature would not be enough of a cover.

"And chew a stick of gum," Jingle suggested in her light

voice. Her eyelids and lips were already glittering with silver sparkles for the club. She smiled up from her laptop and pinched Tiny's round cheek. "No pre-teen smells quite so nicotine addled."

"Did Flip have any success finding out what's going on out there?" Seethe asked, after swilling a mouthful of his beer. "Why things are stirred up right now?"

"No," Hato's face was grim. "He's also had no luck finding that 'Raze' expert Miss Lotus recommended when he was in Japan."

"The name 'Raze' isn't much to go by," Trix grimaced. "Especially if that's the only thing even Miss Lotus really knows about him in the way of contact details."

"Flip's heard some pretty mad stories about this guy," Quicklips stated. "And I heard things back in Mexico too. He would be an asset."

Jingle shrugged. "I tried searching for him online. There are stories from all over. But he would of course go by different names too, and I can't find a pattern to pin him down. Too many Raze rumours without concrete sightings."

"We'll go on as best we can as we are," Hato replied. "Start has drawn up some routes on the map for tonight at least." Hato nodded at where Start was setting out his laminated poster, which had red marker on it. "He's worked out which directions the worst hits seem to be coming from. And soon we might just narrow down where a base could be."

Kid stopped paying them any attention as they worked out which streets Frazzle, Start and Hato would cover on their bikes.

Kiddo grimaced as he stared at the foamy bubbles in the

sink, sloshing plates and glasses clean with a cloth. One element of dinner had not been a great success.

Potato mash. Undercooked. He'd got distracted by the microwave, by the dryer finishing its load, and by a receipt that he'd forgotten to pencil into the budget book. The potato mash had turned out lumpy. And most of the group had left it on their plates.

He half missed the rack now, clanking a glass down to dry too noisily.

More butter. More mashing. Next time. And he hadn't finished folding that load. Because the receipt system needed to be better. He needed to –

Kid felt a strong hand frame his jaw and tilt his face to the side so that he was facing Hato instead of phasing out over the bubbly water.

A bowl dropped back into the sink with a splash.

"You have dark circles under your eyes again," Hato stated coolly.

"He always does," Sparks grinned, swatting Hato's hard grip away, and patting Kid on the cheek. She gave a pointed glance toward where Kid had let the dishwashing liquid tip over. He quickly righted the bottle and stooped to mop up the slowly growing green slick.

Sparks was the group's mechanic and weapons master. She was down to earth. And she was Kid's favourite. She described her style as 'classic grease monkey', with her preference being for blue overalls and black tank tops that Kid always went the extra mile to iron out.

She was tough, like the others. And once he'd seen her booting someone's teeth in before his very eyes. But she was a gentle soul, especially toward him, and Kiddo always saw her as if she were surrounded in a hero's glow.

"Well?" Hato pushed.

"Up late," Kid muttered, eyes down as he wiped at the last of the puddle. "Talking to your newbie."

"Newbie?" Hato frowned. "We don't have anyone new, or any guests at the moment. You taking your meds?" Hato pulled Kid back upright by his arm, and peered into his eyes.

"Yes," Kid pushed Hato's rough hand away again defensively.

"Then get more sleep tonight," Hato ordered. "And good grades tomorrow."

"Kiddo found that fault with the c-gars the other day," Sparks looped her arm through Hato's and led him away. Kid blew upward at his fringe in relief.

"He took one apart," Sparks went on.

"He was probably fidgeting and daydreaming," Hato rumbled dourly.

"*And*," Sparks ignored him. "We noticed they had stiff trigger connectors."

"Did he manage to put it all back together again?" Seethe smirked.

The group slowly made their way out of the living space and up the stairwell to the sleeping quarters to get decked out for the night.

"Those shooters aren't cheap," Seethe added.

"Course he did," Sparks lied, her voice disappearing as the warehouse door slid closed.

Kid had got distracted, swivelling on her wheelie chair

while watching her work to fix the other c-gars, and then to service the team's vehicles that night. His c-gar had been left in a pile.

She'd had grease streaks on her forearms, and her short hair had been falling from its tie as she'd leaned under the bonnet of a car. She was the most beautiful thing he had ever seen. And it was always easy to phase out over her.

Kiddo glanced down at the still mostly full sink. Glowering at how easy it seemed to phase out over the bubbles too.

Once he finished the half done dishes, the less than half done folding and the almost finished budget, he resolved to put the c-gar back in shape.

He had to wipe where Seethe's boots had been too.

And shit! Feed Duncan Jr. The fish.

| 3 |

Three

The pulsing throbs of the music thumping from the underground club were audible from the ground level – the garage and training rooms.

With each pulsation from The Lair, Sparks' tools jangled and jumped where they rested.

Kid didn't mind. The muted chaos radiating up through the floor, thumping under his shoes, made his leg jitter and his head bounce in time. It all reflected the jumpiness he always felt inside.

He clipped the last piece into place, quickly and efficiently soldering it together permanently.

Then he pushed off with his wheelie chair, launching down the long aisles of cars and bikes and skidding to a stop at the firing range part of where the training room began.

"Noise, noise, noise," he muttered, walking the last steps to an empty stall and twirling the gun.

Rocking back and forth on his feet, he squinted at the target down the end of the run, and then fired off five accurate shots in quick succession.

He whistled between his teeth, checking the weapon still looked in good shape under the pressure.

"Fixed it," he congratulated himself, rocking back on his feet.

"And you sure killed that silhouette poster," another voice congratulated. "But I thought you didn't find violence very fun?"

Kid whirled, eyes narrowed, gun ready.

The stranger was seated in the wheelie chair that Kid had left empty. His elbows on his knees, leaning forward to watch the show.

"I did say I don't enjoy it," Kid said quietly. "I didn't say I'm not good at it."

"Ah," the stranger nodded. "I see."

Kiddo could see a red welt-like scar twisting like a flame behind the stranger's ear, met by the lines of a tattoo on the left side of the stranger's neck, but it was too hidden by his collar to make it out.

"It's not a great idea to sneak up on a guy with a gun and a precise shot," Kid went on. He felt the heat of adrenaline rushing in his veins, in time to the music thumps from below.

"It seems you would be right," the stranger agreed, still totally unbothered. "But you wouldn't want to make a bloody mess for Sparks in here."

"Hato said we have no guests. You're probably not real," Kid shrugged. "Sleep deprived brain and all. I conjured you up."

"You did well, then," the stranger said amiably. "I'm very detailed. And you've put me in my favourite jacket each night."

Kid scowled. "You're not that detailed. My brain hasn't even given you a name."

"Dom."

"Dom?"

"There you go. A name. And Hato is wrong – he does have a guest, and I am very real."

"Dom …" Kid put the safety on and placed the gun on a nearby bench. He leaned on the bench distractedly. He had heard that name before.

He was certain Dom was one of Hato's friends. An old one, from way back.

"Why're you here talking to me again?" Kiddo asked. "Instead of hanging out with Hato or helping the gang?"

"I've been helping in my own way," Dom waved a hand. "And they're not as interesting as you."

Kid realised he'd picked up a small screwdriver, and was twirling it over his fingers. He put it down.

"Interesting case," Kid folded his arms and arched an eyebrow. "Great."

"Oh, the whole gang *is* interesting, if you don't feel like flattering yourself," Dom reassured him. He lifted his weight for a second and swivelled the chair so that he could drape his arms over the headrest as he sat. "Hato's collection."

"A rag tag group of kids that he saved from the streets," Kid asserted, feeling the need to defend the tough leader.

"Skilled individuals to use in his own way," Dom smiled. "Such as making you do the bookwork."

"I pull my weight," Kid retorted. "It's only fair. Are you two even friends?"

"Well, we go way back," Dom mused. "I know him well enough to get in here. But he'll definitely be surprised to see me."

"In a good way?"

"Sure," Dom replied easily, wheeling himself closer to inspect Kid's discarded c-gar. "Great work on this, by the way."

"How far back exactly do you and Hato go?"

Dom rubbed his chin. "Let's see. We ran the streets together when I was eight. Hato was fourteen. Seethe was there too – already angry at the world at fifteen."

It was a similar story for most of them.

But Hato was only twenty-four now, and he had built himself up enough to be able to get other promising kids off the streets. Kid was lucky not to have been out in the wild for long.

Kid shifted his weight, frowning in thought.

"Get comfortable," Dom encouraged. "The night is young compared to our last meeting."

"I'm never comfortable," Kid admitted dryly, hoisting himself up onto the work bench and fiddling with a spanner. "My head is full of fireworks and my body's full of spasms."

"Yet you are still a treat."

Kid peered doubtfully down at himself. He couldn't even say that he'd loosened his school tie and top buttons to relax. That was his normal state. Sloppy and untucked. It drove his teachers mad.

That and the constant window staring, pen clicking and chewing, chairs rocked too far backward and such. The other day the bell had sounded and Kiddo had realised he'd spent most of that session just gnawing on a finger and blinking as he thought.

"Right," Kid remarked sarcastically. "A real treat."

"Well, you see, the others have been easy to peg," Dom explained. "Not you."

"I should be worried."

"No, no," Dom grinned in a way that suggested it should be a yes. "Hato does his research. Before I get back into his life, I want to do the same."

"Spying?"

"Prepping," Dom corrected.

"And what has your spying told you?"

Dom didn't deny it this time. "You guys have a real rat problem in your area," he started smoothly, and he was not referring to actual vermin. "Seethe still loves next to nothing, but he can steal anything. Hato has got even harder, but he can lead anyone. The one you call Tiny is actually like a baby tank. Jingle is sweet, and great with tech. Quicklips could sweet talk a nun and convince the highest court of their injustice. Frazzle is a slow thinker, but clever with his hands."

"He's not a slow thinker," Kid interrupted, squeezing his palms between his knees to keep from tapping his fingers on the bench. "Frazzle's first language is Arabic. He has to think in two languages. And he gets stressed out. PTSD. But he was a medic in Gaza."

"I'll add that to the memory bank," Dom inclined his head in a thank you before moving on. "Flip is scarily good with a switch blade and recon."

Kiddo blinked then. How did Dom know that? Flip had been away chasing the phantom snatcher hunter called Raze.

"Start is a procrastinator, an over thinker, but also a great strategist," Dom continued. "Trix is a mercenary who literally has a million tricks up her sleeve and can think on her feet. Velvet is a sultry little minx who has a penchant for push up bras, and absolutely nobody should cross her. And Sparks can fix anything." Dom cocked his head to regard Kid then. "You, Cayden Kit Lake, have been harder to work out."

"You've made a fair effort in your research anyway," Kiddo said darkly at the use of his full name. He hated to think exactly what scenarios this guy had been watching, to learn those specifics about the gang.

"Oh it's just typical, superficial, on record stuff for you," Dom shrugged that off. "But you keep your mouth shut to the group, your body language is confusing, and your academic results range from outstanding excellence to near fails depending on your mood. Don't get me started on your behaviour record."

Kiddo thunked a spanner down solidly. "I don't know how you've been able to spy on us so closely. But I am leaning more toward Hato's surprise at seeing you being a negative kind of surprise."

"You could be right, come to think of it," Dom tapped his chin. "It could bring back some demons. But anyway. At least I've enjoyed my time with you."

Dom rose much more quickly than any of his other placid movements had been previously. Kiddo was in no way expecting it when the other young man swept toward him in two steps, pushing him backward to lay across the bench.

With one hand holding Kid's chest down, Dom pressed his free fingers to the side of Kid's neck.

"You really do need more sleep," Dom stated, and with a quick shot of movement from his fingers, Kiddo felt the restless pressure leave his body for the first time in as long as he could remember.

His startled eyes closed, his own hands stopped scrabbling to throw off Dom's hold, and his body seemed to sink downward into release.

| 4 |

Four

"Kiddo, I think Hato's working you too hard," Sparks' voice woke him.

Kiddo jolted back to consciousness with a start, only keeping from jumping right out of his skin because of her hand on his chest – much as Dom's had been last night.

"Passing out on a workshop bench isn't ideal," Sparks added a little worriedly, pressing her other hand to his forehead.

Kid shook his brain clear of its fuzziness, quickly sitting up and rubbing at the sore spot on his neck in annoyance.

"You good?" she asked, tucking short, dark hair behind her ear. The ends were tipped with some sort of product that made them spiky. Spunky.

"Fine," he jittered, slipping forward off the bench. "Just a headache. And possible hallucinations," he added under his breath.

"Is it a skip school kind of day?" Sparks had quit school that year. Her final year.

He swore as he grabbed her wrist and saw the time. "It's a

missed the bus on a makeup test kind of day," he groaned. "I'll catch you at dinner!"

He skidded under the garage roller door and sprinted the six blocks it took to get to school. Not surprising anyone when he collapsed into a chair, late, at the back of class, and looking as rumpled in his uniform as ever.

"Automatic detention for tardiness," the teacher scolded, but slapped the paper down in front of him as he gaped for air and wheezed over a stitch. "Focus," the teacher added. As if it were easy.

"Sorry ma'am," he uttered quietly.

He slumped forward over his paper, staring at the font spiralling on his page and escaping over his desk.

If he didn't rein his brain in fast, the letters would fly right out the windows and his makeup test would be worse than the original.

His brain flexed experimentally with flying thoughts ...

Groceries, detention, electricity bill, ace this test, feed Duncan Jr.

Oh yeah, possibly get a head check, and remember to get new meds from the chemist. He was out.

Wait, that was all out of order.

He rubbed his face, squeezing his eyes closed and back open.

With steely effort, he forced his brain to hone in on the words running away from him like water. They wriggled as much as he did. But he caught them, and grasped them, and forced his thoughts to stop and make sense of them.

As if the sun had just shone down on his page, he shook

his head at the simplicity of all of it. He knew every single thing on the page.

A rushed start hadn't helped, but an uncannily sound sleep sure had.

| 5 |

Five

"I missed Kiddo's meals while I was off on my Raze ghost hunt," Flip sighed appreciatively.

"The potatoes were amazing tonight," Trix announced, slapping Kid on the back. She winced then, glaring at her bruised knuckles, and Kid rose to throw her a bag of frozen vegetables from the freezer before starting to clear the table.

"Extra buttery and smooth," Tiny burped appreciatively.

"Unlike *your* efforts to give out a vulnerable sob story last night," Jingle told Tiny primly. "You don't have a subtle bone in your body."

"I had to make it known that I was snatch worthy," Tiny protested. "Or how will we ever notice the interested parties?"

"You were listing it all like you were in an exam," Trix snorted. " *'Oh, I'm so young and alone and helpless. Did I mention nobody would miss me if I was gone?'* "

"Speaking of sloppiness," Hato's hard eyes found Kiddo at the bench, who sighed in acknowledgement of what was coming.

"I got an alert to say you had detention again," Hato went on. "Lateness."

"Well, that's mundane," Seethe commented evilly. "No blood, no foul."

"Kiddo also got full marks for his test," Sparks interjected.

"Heyyyy," Quicklips raised his glass in a toast.

"And he was so tired I found him passed out on a work bench," Sparks added in his defence. "It's lucky he went at all," she finished, only just catching Kiddo's warning look and shake of the head.

"What?" Hato asked in a low voice, eyes narrowing.

Hato often reminded Kiddo of Muhammad Ali in his prime. A force to be reckoned with – even just by death glare.

"Talking to strangers again?" Velvet teased with a little sneer. She was filing her nails to sharp points.

"Talking to your friend. Dom," Kiddo admitted to Hato with a stony face and shrug.

There was silence from the table.

Seethe lowered his beer bottle, and Tiny swallowed his smoke ring.

"You were not talking to Dominic," Hato stated at last.

"Black hair, combed back. As tall as me," Kiddo said. "Lean muscle. Pale skin. Slick. Part of a tattoo on his neck. Knows everyone here so well he must have been watching the place for weeks."

"It was *not* Dominic," Seethe hissed, as if that was that.

"You've mentioned his name once or twice in the past," Jingle said uncertainly. "Why mightn't a childhood friend come to visit?"

"Because," Seethe said through gritted teeth. "He's dead."

Kiddo saw Hato's face blanche.

Frazzle bowed his head respectfully.

Start for once actually got started on something other than his maps – quickly picking up a pamphlet from the junk mail pile.

"So, Kiddo's lost it," Velvet mused. "Or he's drinking again."

"No," Quicklips puzzled over it for a moment. "I'm sure I've seen a past photo of Seethe and Hato with this Dom guy, from before they were snatched. Kiddo must have caught sight of it when he was cleaning up after you lot."

"Then his tired mind made a dream of it," Sparks agreed reassuringly.

"Dominic would have been a kid in any photos of us," Seethe said less reassuringly. "Not quite the image he's describing here."

"You taking your meds?" Hato asked stiffly.

"Yes," Kid lied. He'd remembered to ace his test, detention, groceries, Duncan Jr. and to pay that bill. This counted as that head check he'd considered.

But he had not remembered to stop at the drug store.

"Did you get more sleep last night?"

"Yes." Not a lie.

"Do the same thing tonight," Hato ordered. "And we'll all work out a better game plan so that Tiny doesn't get us sprung." He turned to Start, and motioned for the usual planning over the laminated poster map to begin.

The matter was closed.

Kiddo felt the angst and heightened energy drop from his shoulders.

Until he remembered that he seemed to be speaking to ghosts.

| 6 |

Six

Jumping out of his skin as the unchecked ADHD jerked its way through every nerve, Kiddo could hardly do up his zip.

His head was pounding. But he bunched and then un-bunched his fingers, making them work, and then pulled his hood up.

The hyperactivity he could handle. Those pills just offered a sweet little bit of stimulant to tone him down or boost him up in the right ways. So that he didn't feel like he was a messy child's picture that had been coloured outside the lines.

But the headaches, the out of body sensation, and the metallic taste that was creeping up on him … as well as hallu-cinations of dead guys. Well, they didn't bode well.

"Where you goin?"

Kiddo stopped rattling his way down the warehouse stairs at once.

Quicklips had popped his head up from where he'd been sprawled out on the couch on the living level. An anonymous woman, half his great size, was fast asleep with her head on his chest. Her glittery disco dress was a slippery looking pile on the floor.

"Forgot something at the store," Kiddo answered.

"Nope." Quicklips shook his head. "Wait til tomorrow. I can even take you."

Kiddo rattled down a few more steps. "I can take care of myself. I won't be long."

"I know you can," Quicklips answered. "But your night jaunts are off the table while things are getting so tense on the streets. The snatchers are right riled up about something big happening."

Kiddo gritted his teeth, his knuckles tapping rapidly against the banister. But he gave a quick nod, and then launched himself back up the stairs.

He thundered up to try to pass through the private quarters again quickly, but a hand snaked out of the nearest bedroom doorway, and pulled him off the stairs by the collar.

"Where you off to?" Seethe drawled, flicking his pale gaze up toward the library, where Kiddo had been planning to head.

Kiddo would have made straight for the door to the outside fire escape, with access to the rooftop garden, or access to the streets below – if you knew the right steps to avoid Jingle's threshold sensors.

"Forgot a book up there," Kiddo tried.

Seethe scratched the light patch of hair on his bare chest, releasing Kiddo's collar to lean in his open bedroom doorway.

Seethe's usual, cool glare always held suspicion and distrust, but he was regarding Kiddo with especially narrowed eyes.

"Forget the book. Go to bed."

Kiddo couldn't help but scoff. "Since when is anyone home at this hour and caring about bedtimes?"

"Since it's my night off, and since Hato said you might need a baby-sitter if you're going through a weird phase. Naturally, I am the perfect nurturing choice."

Seethe rotated Kiddo where he stood, and gave him a shove between the shoulder blades, back in the direction of his own room down the hall.

"Fine," Kid muttered, rubbing at his temples before closing his door.

But sleeping was out of the question, while a quick walk to the chemist was very necessary. He needed those other meds so that this 'weird phase' would get under control.

He turned from the closed door and kept walking to his window, easing it open. A cloud of misty rain blew in at once.

"Course it's wet," Kiddo muttered to himself.

Then, with practiced ease, he slipped out, swung from the pipe along the wall, and landed on the fire escape stairs a couple of meters from his window.

He stepped lightly, sometimes sliding his way down the rails of the multi-story warehouse stairwell, until his sneakers touched down on the pavement.

Slouching in his hoody, with hands jammed in his denim pockets against the rain, he took the back streets toward the twenty-four-hour chemist.

Right as he got into view of the drug-store's green neon sign at the end of his alley, he heard the sounds of footfalls.

Heightened senses whirring, he could tell it was too many

footfalls for it to be just another forgetful customer hurrying through the dark to purchase their fix.

"Ah shit," Kid scowled, and stopped. Halfway through the alley.

His gaze flicked to the drugstore dumpster, and he hurriedly crossed to grab an offcut steel pole; maybe a piece of scaffolding, dumped from the street.

He was twirling it experimentally as three figures became apparent in the green light ahead, obscured by the rolling clouds of rain.

He wasn't surprised to see two more of them step in to seal off the other side of the alley behind him. They were even harder to see in the dark. But they all wore balaclavas with the image of bloodied fangs printed across the mouths.

Snatchers.

Hato would be pissed. Quicklips would be betrayed. Seethe would be seething. And Kiddo would be gone without a trace.

Ahh geeze. Sparks would think he was an idiot. After all their gang knew about the snatchers.

"Keep his face pretty," one guy hissed. "This one's a ten."

"And keep the body intact," another agreed from the other side of him as they closed in. "Nothing long term."

"The usual," a very bulky figure grunted. "You sure are *lovely*," he told Kiddo, in the least complimentary way possible. "Which Asian flavour are you?"

Kiddo put his back toward a brick wall, twisting the offcut pole in his hands.

"I'll be missed," Kid promised. "My disappearance won't be quiet."

"We saw you come from the place above The Lair. That little guy drilled into us last night that those kids have no legal guardians. So sad. So alone."

"You'll slip through the cracks."

"The news will say: a runaway. Off wasting the system's time. Off the rails. No hoper. Not missed."

Man, had they read Kid's personal record? Had Tiny used Kiddo for inspiration?

"I do make some bad choices," Kiddo agreed in his low voice, his heart thumping as much as his brain. "And look, off to buy drugs. I'm pretty faulty."

"Not for what the buyers will want you for."

"You'll fetch a good price with those looks."

"You could be our prized winner."

"I'll be expensive to keep, with those regular drug needs and all," Kiddo warned without much hope, watching as they closed a half circle around him, backing him closer to the wall.

"Then they'll add you to the gladiator matches, or they'll dispose of you."

"And pay again for a new toy."

"Either way, you've just topped off this week's quota."

They launched forward at once, well-practiced in wrangling struggling youths who had the drive and energy of fighting for their lives.

He got in two good swings, swiping one across the head with a satisfying and resounding musical note from the pole, and heard another clang as he hit the knees of a second one.

There were curses as the other three came at Kid with arms that darted from everywhere, jabbing him in the ribs, slugging him in the stomach and driving at his own legs as someone wrenched the pole from his fingers.

He fought like a wildcat, catching one snatcher around the neck and dragging the guy along with him as he sank down – winded and battered continually as they targeted his sides.

Someone got in another blow to his stomach so that he lost his suffocating grip on the guy, before there was a surprised yowl from one of Kid's other attackers, and Dom materialised – having leapt onto the masked figure's back.

With a fast crack to the assailant's neck, Dom rode the now slack body downward, before darting forward to rip a snatcher off Kiddo's chest. The snatcher hurtled backward, and Dom propelled him for added force, as hard as possible into the brick wall. There was a crunch and a yelp, before the masked menace slid downward.

Kiddo aimed a fist into the cheekbone of the other guy still holding him down. And Dom was just coming back to grab Kiddo's now swaying attacker by the armpits, ready to crush this one's face too, when someone recovered enough to hit Dom hard across the head with Kiddo's lost pole.

The taut energy and calculated awareness that had made Dom so fierce suddenly evaporated, and he crumpled downward like a tower of blocks losing form.

Kiddo grunted as he was hauled up onto his feet and thrown against the wall. The cold of the wet bricks seeped into his shoulder blades, and two now less sharply moving snatchers came forward to try to work fast.

One pinned a forearm across Kiddo's gullet, while the other leaned down to grab for his wrists to cable-tie them.

With a fast jab, Kiddo caught the leaning snatcher with a hard poke to the eyes that set the man to screaming at once. With a quick stomp to the foot, Kiddo had his strangler inching his forearm back a little from Kiddo's throat – giving enough space for Kiddo to deliver a spectacular rabbit punch to the man's groin.

"How do *you* like it?" Dom was back in the game, getting ready to club someone with the pole now himself.

There was swearing, and flailing, and the three still upright snatchers seemed to be pulling back in a limping kind of retreat. Backing their way toward the green neon light after getting more than they'd bargained for.

Seizing the opportunity, Kiddo grabbed Dom's wrist and yanked him into a full sprint in the opposite direction and right out of the alleyway. The pole clanged to the ground as it slipped from Dom's fingers as he tried to keep up.

Kiddo had to make them disappear fast, but Dom was lagging. He likely couldn't see straight.

Ribs burning and his own head pulsing like the music from The Lair, Kiddo kept his grip on Dom, and forced them to run like shooting arrows through the back streets and toward the outer docks.

| 7 |

Seven

He wrenched Dom toward a wire fence, barely stopping as he led the way up and over it so that Dom had to follow.

Then he dragged Dom over mossy rocks, skidding downward, into a concrete, industrial tunnel with sloshing sea water protecting one entrance, and the fence in view from the other.

Dom crashed in after Kiddo, who caught him before they both toppled all the way out into the bay.

"You good?" Kiddo asked, gripping Dom by the arms and pushing him upright.

"Hey, *I* was trying to be the saviour," Dom protested, waving the finger with the lotus tattoo. "*You* good?"

Kiddo pushed his sopping fringe out of his eyes, peering at the red darts of blood combining with the water droplets that were running down Dom's face. Watery blood was rolling over the red mark behind Dom's ear, where the other tattoo began.

"Ahh, man. That cut looks nasty," Kiddo grimaced.

"Ahh, man. My head sure hurts," Dom agreed tiredly, his

chin tilting toward his chest as he shivered. His lips were purple.

Kiddo gripped Dom's chin and titled it back up so that Dom's eyes refocused on him. "Stay awake. We only need to stay here until they stop waiting for me to go home. Hato and Velvet are patrolling on their bikes, so the snatchers shouldn't hang around too long."

Dom nodded, shuddering, his teeth chattering. And Kiddo quickly looped an arm around Dom's shoulders. He could feel the tremors rippling Dom's body against his own.

"It'll be right," Kiddo promised.

"They saw where you come from?" Dom asked.

"Must have been watching the club for Tiny to be unprotected. Made himself too appealing last night. But they got me instead."

"They might not hang around tonight," Dom warned. "But there are other nights. And word spreads about a ten."

"I should be flattered," Kiddo said flatly. "Never considered myself a ten."

"Sure you are," Dom complimented. "Closest thing to an eleven I've ever seen. Very unlucky for you."

"Hato is going to be mad."

"Understatement."

Kiddo turned to peer at the gash on Dom's forehead. It was a purple, bleeding split that rent from eyebrow to hairline.

"That's going to need stitches."

"They don't give up on tens," Dom sighed. "Even when you're not a ten, you have to die before they'll consider losing the money they could make if they've set their sights on you."

"Do you want me to get you to a hospital when we know we're clear?" Kiddo persisted.

"No," Dom answered firmly. "Nowhere gets a record of me. I'm a ghost."

Kiddo grimaced. "I'd just reassured myself that you weren't."

"You have to die before they'll stop looking for you," Dom said pointedly. "So I did."

Kiddo's eyebrows rose. "I see."

"Took a real risk showing myself to help you out," Dom went on. "And now it turns out I've probably slowed you down."

"I would have taken to the rooftops and lost them in the getaway," Kiddo admitted. He would likely have been pulling himself back through his window right now. Safe within Jingle's sensor covered fortress. "But I wasn't giving them the slip without your help in the first place."

"Mmm." Dom's cheek was on Kiddo's shoulder now.

"Hey, eyes open," Kiddo shook Dom's shoulders.

"Yep," Dom blinked his head back up. "Wide."

"I had got the impression you were a pretty placid person," Kiddo started – trying to keep Dom talking. He shivered a little himself as he remembered the neck snapping. It was hard to reconcile with the young man blinking sleepily in his arms.

"Oh, I'm very placid," Dom answered agreeably. "I've spent a long time forcing my head back into a working state of calm. But," he lifted his shoulders a little. "I'd watched you walking in the rain, hands in pockets, wouldn't hurt a fly. Disappearing down an alley and not coming back out."

Kiddo rolled his eyes. "Spy." He huffed. "As I told you, I

don't find violence very fun, but that doesn't mean I'm not good at it."

"I actually did know that," Dom admitted. "Two schools ago, you had that incident with the bullies. Read all about it."

"They were flushing that first year's head," Kiddo defended.

"Sounds like they didn't know what was coming their way," Dom chuckled.

"I can't stand bullies," Kiddo stated sourly. That was one reason Kid had actually stuck with Hato and the gang, when no happy families type foster house had felt right. It was because the gang was ultimately all about sticking up for the little guys, and keeping them safe from the big bads.

"You're keeping your head down at this school though?" Dom asked. "Keeping your cool."

Kiddo leaned forward to check the fence's rattling sounds were because of the wind. He swallowed a metallic taste on his tongue.

"Hato and the others try to keep me in check with a semi-normal life and routine," he answered. "When they found me, I thought I was a party animal. But I was just an animal. Slurring and stumbling, and an easy target."

"What were you celebrating? You would have only been about thirteen?"

Kiddo winced. "I was killing myself slowly, in my own way. Burning through brain cells. Trying to stay awake and at the same time deaden everything I was living through. I don't drink now. I don't even do sugar."

"Why? Teenagers love sugar, don't they?" Dom's voice

was getting fuzzy, so Kiddo thought it was time to get moving again.

He angled himself past Dom, and backed out of the tunnel, pulling Dom out too by the lapels of his leather jacket.

At least the rain had let up.

"ADHD," Kiddo explained. "I can't contain myself on a normal day. Imagine me jacked up on kilojoules."

"Your file had a little medical symbol," Dom mused. "But it was restricted." He let Kiddo throw Dom's arm over his shoulders, and wrap his other arm around Dom's waist. He was slightly taller than Kiddo.

"So you don't know *everything* then," Kiddo teased, walking them along the docks to get home from a different way. He was taking a fair bit of Dom's weight.

"You are a beautiful mystery," Dom promised. "I came for Hato and to suss out the gang. But you are kind of on the outskirts of what they're about, while also intrinsically part of who they all are."

"Think you're giving me more credit than is due," Kid told him dryly.

"Hato sees you as the glue," Dom explained. "You are the thing that made them start to behave more like a family. The kid they want to do well. But I didn't expect that, when I read your file. I thought you would be well on your way to becoming a Seethe."

"Loving nothing, fighting everything?" Kiddo asked. He supposed if he'd kept up his street life, or even his resentment toward the foster homes, he would have become Seethe.

"He doesn't hate you," Dom corrected. "He loves all of you, and what you've all got."

"Loves?" Kiddo scoffed, taking an off street that would start angling them back in toward the warehouse.

"In his own way," Dom affirmed. "He doesn't want you to become him. Filled with poison. Hato has you pegged for making a real life for yourself. Winning awards for your brains. Proving things can be better."

"That's a lot of pressure," Kiddo grumbled.

"Meanwhile, you patiently take care of them, and you keep to the outside of things, while taking on the best traits of all of them."

"Right," Kiddo squinted out across the road that divided them from the warehouse now. Clear of the gang's patrolling bikes … apparently clear of less friendly watchers too. He tightened his grip on his new friend, and pushed off – moving them fast across the open road.

"Hato's survival skills," Dom panted – wincing as his head was jolted. "Velvet's smarts – you're less conniving though, mind you. Seethe's clever toughness – less klepto though, thankfully. Quicklips' charm …"

"You think I'm charming." Kiddo dragged Dom up along the fire escape stairs.

"You ashamed to show me off to the family honey?" Dom questioned in return with a grin.

"You don't want to give Hato that surprise of first seeing you when he's angry. Not when you're in this state," Kiddo explained. "Best they don't know I was gone."

"Best they know they have a ten on their hands."

"When I'm ready."

"Alriiight … You have the glint of steel about you that Flip and Tiny have. You have the cleverness of Trix and Start. Also the sweetness of Jingle. And you're down to earth like Sparks."

"I'm too jumpy to be down to earth like Sparks," Kiddo disagreed wistfully.

He'd got them up to his bedroom window level now, and he was eyeing the wet pipe and open space they'd have to swing to get to the window.

In Dom's shape, the door to the library would be better. But if a sensor was tripped or the others caught sight of Kiddo with Dom, there would be hell to pay.

"I'm good," Dom promised. "Still nimble if I focus."

"Focus is easier said than done sometimes," Kiddo replied slowly, deliberating. He didn't really want to watch Dom drop to his death.

"I've got this," Dom assured. "But then I'm taking a nap."

"No, then I'm raiding Frazzle's first aid stuff," Kiddo disagreed.

"As you wish," Dom gestured for Kiddo to go first.

Letting Dom take his own weight, and making sure he wasn't going to sway right over the rails, Kiddo climbed up to reach for the pipe, using all of the strength of his forearms, and what little grip his sneakers could get on the wet walls, to lever himself across the distance to the window.

His ribs were burning as he used his core to help him get up and in, before he turned in time to catch Dom lithely swinging in after him.

"See?" Dom delivered a smile before stumbling over to

crawl on the slightly damp bed. "Nimble in even the worst of times."

"As it turns out," Kiddo admitted. "Don't go to sleep."

"Teenagers love sleep, though. Don't they?" Dom murmured as Kiddo slipped from the room.

| 8 |

Eight

Dom's eyes were wild and Kiddo had to catch his fist as Dom woke with guns blazing.

It took a second, his chest heaving, before his face softened with recognition.

"That stung," Dom accused.

"You went to sleep," Kiddo returned calmly. He continued dabbing at the wound over Dom' eyebrow with his disinfectant soaked cloth.

"And you haven't," Dom sighed. "Another night with not enough z's clocked up for you. Want me to do that trick again?"

"No," Kiddo stated flatly. "My neck is still tight from that, thank you."

"I could fix that," Dom offered.

"No." Very flat this time. "I've seen what else you can do to necks."

"Ah." Dom winced as Kiddo blew on the gash to dry it. "Never to yours though. I have trust issues, but when I find my kind of person, I keep them alive."

"How do you know I'm your kind of person?"

Dom watched without any doubts in his expression as Kiddo turned to where he had lined up a tray on the bedside table. There was a sterilised curved needle with a long nylon thread on the tray, along with scissors.

"All those wonderful traits mentioned earlier are part of it," Dom answered. He didn't seem phased that Kiddo had to shake out his twitching fingers before he could hold the delicate needle steady.

It wasn't nerves. Frazzle had taught Kiddo to help treat minor wounds, like when suturing was needed, if someone in the gang needed patching.

Kiddo had a lot of time for Frazzle, who was jumpy and all over the place in the head too. But, also because Frazzle managed to work past those things, and tolerantly treated the most dangerous, whiney or grumpy of patients in their group. He'd even loaned Kiddo his English based medical journals for night time reading on many occasions – one of which Kiddo had just consulted for a quick refresher.

"Too much energy," Kiddo muttered to himself in annoyance, forcing his leg to stop bouncing, and rolling his neck and shoulders to try to get the jitters out.

"I like that about you too," Dom grinned. "You're such a mix."

"Oh?" Kiddo leaned in over Dom with now much steadier hands. He made a holding stitch at the edge of the wound closest to the brow, and Dom groaned loudly.

"Shh!" Kiddo covered Dom's mouth with his free hand, pushing him back against the pillows.

He glared down sternly.

Dom gave a nod, and Kiddo felt Dom's lips quirk before he slowly let go his hold.

"I'll be good," Dom whispered devilishly. "Quiet as a mouse."

Taking a deep breath, Kiddo went on with his continuous line as efficiently as possible.

It would have been painful, but Dom managed to let Kiddo pull his skin together into a neat line, now free of the risk of infection, without emitting another peep.

He simply watched Kiddo work over him, with dark blue eyes on Kiddo's face, and his lips clamped firmly shut until Kiddo was snipping the excess thread away.

"Thank you," Dom stated, while Kiddo blotted the neat line with disinfectant again, and applied some gauze.

Kiddo slid his bedside drawer open and a near empty pain killer bottle rolled into sight. He popped the cap and shook two free.

"Swallow those. They'll help," he instructed Dom, and grabbed two for himself, passing Dom a half filled glass of water left forgotten on a book shelf.

It was the first time in a while that Kiddo remembered his own marks of battle, and more concerningly, the increasingly pounding headache that warned him he really needed to get to that drug store in the morning.

"Hope you know I couldn't get off this bed if I tried," Dom announced luxuriously. "I'm energy depleted."

"Take some of mine," Kid quipped acerbically. He unzipped his hoodie and gingerly drew his t-shirt over his head, putting them straight in the wash pile.

"They've got to be sore," Dom commented, regarding the bruising already flourishing up and down Kiddo's sides.

"I'm guessing we've both survived worse," Kiddo shook it off, examining himself for a second. "I wouldn't have been getting in that window if they were broken or anything too terrible had happened."

"You're a ten, remember?" Dom pointed out. He rubbed at where a tattoo and red lines ran from behind his ear to down his neck and collar. "They wanted to incapacitate you without doing lasting damage to your looks."

"Beauty is a blessing and a curse," Kid scowled, and made room for himself next to Dom, putting his arms behind his head to stare at the ceiling.

Snatchers were almost the least of his worries, if he didn't remember to get to that chemist. He had to get up early to make it there before school.

"I think you're fine to sleep now," Kiddo told Dom then. "I'll wake you in a couple of hours when I need to get ready for school and check you don't seem too dazed or confused. If that happens, though," he said seriously, "you're off to hospital – ghost or not."

He started to make himself a mental list. Wake up early, check Dom's mental capacity, grab the shopping list, get to the chemist, do not miss the bus, avoid another late detention, a test was on in the morning, get home, make a great dinner that might somehow soften the news that he was a 'ten', feed Duncan Jr, start a paper that was due after the weekend, and make an order on low stocks for The Lair. If he finished his paper early, he could spend some time helping Sparks with the cars. Watching her do her thing ...

"You gonna sleep?" Dom asked, already closing his eyes.

"Hope not." Kiddo had already shifted his legs restlessly three times.

Dom leaned up on his elbow. "You got problems Cayden Lake."

"Yup."

Dom tilted forward and pressed his lips to Kiddo's collar bone, and then against his jawline.

"I like girls," Kiddo told him calmly. "Your kisses good-night won't work for me."

"I know," Dom licked his lips. "I like girls too. So I won't hold it against you."

Kiddo raised his eyebrows.

"Sparks is a good example," Dom smiled wickedly.

"Not that one." Kid's eyebrows were straight back down.

"I even like Velvet," Dom went on.

"You said she was conniving," Kiddo accused.

"She is," Dom nodded. "I like that about her. I *get* that about her."

"Ahuh," Kiddo shifted again restlessly.

"But I like you too."

"You said I wasn't so conniving," Kiddo reminded him.

"Oh, I like you for a few reasons. That mix of things I mentioned before," Dom replied airily.

He reached out and hooked a hand around Kiddo's neck as if he might draw him in for a proper goodnight kiss after all. Kiddo wasn't even sure he minded.

"What mix of things?" he asked curiously.

"Tell you tomorrow," Dom told him sweetly. And with a

squeeze at that pressure point in Kiddo's neck, it was lights out.

| 9 |

Nine

Kiddo felt himself surfacing as if from under the weight of a lot of water.

What *was* that?

He sat bolt upright, his usual zaps of energy surging down his arms and legs and to his finger and toe tips.

It was his alarm … which had apparently been sounding off to wake him for twenty minutes.

"Shit," he hissed, launching up off the bed and remembering his ribs with another curse.

He silenced the alarm as he remembered Dom now too.

"Shit, shit, shit."

He practically tore his jeans off, half tripping into his school trousers.

Lucky nature had showered him last night, because that would have to do.

"Hey," he flew to Dom's side, squeezing Dom's wrist.

He ducked the automatic punch he had a feeling Dom would be throwing, and then rushed back to his closet to fish out a white shirt.

"You still sane?" he asked the wild-eyed Dom, turning back as he tried to button the shirt and missed half the holes.

He threw on a tie anyway.

"Hardly," Dom managed, blinking violet eyes and taking in where he was and what was happening as Kiddo pulled on his shoes.

"Perfect," Kiddo panted. "Normal then. Catch you later."

Dom was still sleep mussed and collapsing back against the pillows as Kiddo closed the door and hurtled down the stairs.

"You slept in," Tiny's grumpy reprimand followed him downward as he passed the kitchen.

He ran through the list in his head again:

Wake up early. No.

Check Dom's mental capacity. Kind of.

Grab the shopping list. Shit … he didn't have time to get back to the living level now.

Get to the chemist. No. he'd have to do that later. Like he would *really* have to do that later.

Do not miss the bu – Shit!

Kiddo skidded out onto the pavement to watch the back of the bus disappearing down the street.

If he ran faster than he ever had before, he still might avoid another late detention and make it to the morning test without issue…

He sprinted the six blocks it took to get to school. Yet again not surprising anyone when he collapsed into a chair, late, at the back of class, and looking as rumpled as ever.

"You don't get extra time for being late," the teacher

scolded, slapping the test down in front of him. "But you do get an automatic detention for tardiness. Now focus," the teacher added. As if it were easy.

"Sorry ma'am."

Kiddo bit into his knuckles and glared at his paper, scaring every single number back into place so that his pumping brain could try to make sense of them.

When he finally emerged from the campus gate that afternoon, rubbing his temples, he felt like he had just come out of the other end of another fight with the snatchers.

"Sore head?" a cheerful voice sympathised. "There's a nice pill bottle beside your bed that can help that."

Kiddo whirled, squinting to find Dom, seated casually on a thick, fancy school entrance pillar.

"Hop down," he groaned, unable to bear gazing up at Dom in the light. He'd half come to associate Dom with the night anyway.

"You're the last student out, I think," Dom commented brightly, levering himself off the pillar.

"Detention. Again," Kiddo glowered.

"Tsk tsk."

"Somebody made me sleep through the alarm," Kid growled.

"Somebody thought you needed the sleep," Dom ambled along easily as Kid made his way to the grocery store.

"What are you doing here anyway?" Kid asked with only slightly less annoyance.

"Told you," Dom answered, hands in his pockets. "Once I find my kind of people, I try to keep them alive. You going to tell the gang about your particular snatcher issue?"

Kiddo grimaced. "I need to stop in at the grocery and drug stores first," he remembered his list. "Make a great dinner to soften them up. Feed Duncan Jr. Start a paper that's due Monday. Then make an order on low stocks for The Lair."

"And perve on Sparks in the garage," Dom added helpfully. "You said that when I first put you to sleep."

Kid shoved Dom so hard in the arm that he skipped forward a few steps, laughing.

"Want me to do the groceries while you go into the chemist?" Dom held his hands up in a truce. "Where's the list?"

Kiddo scowled. "I forgot the list."

"Ah well," Dom said. "Off the cuff it is."

Dom trailed him up and down the supermarket aisles, pointing out every useless product that Kiddo could ever possibly not need. But he was very supportively carrying an armful of heavy bags when Kiddo stopped short at the front of the chemist.

"Off on a half hour break, huh?" Dom read the sign.

"Mmm." Kiddo was disgruntled, and getting a little desperate.

"We can wait?" Dom suggested. "Snatchers mostly snatch when it's less busy and at night. We've got plenty of crowd and light right now."

So much light. It was throwing off Kiddo's vision. His head was swimming.

He stared at the sign with the clock picture on it.

The hands on the clock were frozen in place, but the numbers started to look like they were rotating backwards.

It was all getting too frustrating and tiresome. It would be so easy to dump his bags and just wander off to be left alone. Or break a window, pop a whole handful of pain killers and just enjoy this time with a friend who actually sort of got him.

"Did you want to wait?" Dom asked.

"What?" Kiddo shook himself. The taste of metal was in his mouth.

No. Clinging to his jobs and routines had got him much further than instant gratification ever had.

"The roast takes about an hour to cook," Kiddo sighed. "I need to get back and prep."

"Sure thing," Dom replied happily, starting off down the street. "It'll be easier to try the chemist again tomorrow, between your homework and perving, with it being the weekend and all."

"So you're coming back with me, to reveal your non-ghost status?" Kiddo tried to concentrate on Dom, instead of on things he couldn't do anything about.

He found that Dom was magnetic enough to hone his focus in on.

"How about I wait in your room and let you do your buttering up of the gang first." Dom rearranged a bag that was cutting into his wrist. "Then you can tell them all about how I heroically helped you, and they'll be so glad to see me."

"They'll forget about all of your spying?"

"Preparing."

"What I'm about to do to the food is preparing," Kiddo negated. "You were being a little peeping Dom."

Dom chuckled. "Sometimes it wasn't even intentional."

"Now how is that possible?"

"Oh," Dom threw him a grin. "I would fall asleep in one of

Sparks' cars, or be chilling in the ventilation chute over the kitchen, or even just taking some air in the rooftop garden, and my rest stops were where someone would just happen to be."

"You were in those places for the purposes of collecting information and spying in the first place," Kiddo told him.

"And because a guy's got to sleep somewhere," Dom shrugged. "Your bed has been the best spot by far since I got back to town though."

"It being a bed and all."

"As well as it having you in it," Dom nodded.

"What made you decide to talk to me, of all people?" Kiddo asked curiously.

"That wonderful, intriguing mix of things I'd noticed in you," Dom declared openly. "You have this very assertive but also reserved vibe. Like you're wired tight and ready to bubble over all the time, while also being so self-restrained."

Kiddo felt heat flush in his cheeks. "If only you could see the internal mess that that all causes," he muttered. "I feel like I'm constantly on the verge of self-destructing, and one day it'll happen without me even meaning it."

"I can see some of it," Dom nodded. "The night I just couldn't resist talking to you in the library, your legs were sprawled out and also bouncing under that table like you were trying to relax as well as being ready to burst into action at the same time. Your slouch, on the other hand, said you prefer to be under the radar, but you were already firmly on mine."

Kiddo pulled a face. "I am an interesting bug to study."

"I know the movements are just a symptom of what must

be going on in that wonderful head of yours," Dom soothed. "You were doing complicated bookwork with incredible competence. When you put pen to paper, you smashed out two incredibly accurate lines in moments. But in the half hour I'd been watching you before Hato called, you'd done *only* those two lines."

"I went into hyperfocus on it for hours after that," Kiddo admitted. He stared up at the warehouse, surprised at how leisurely he'd allowed their pace to be, considering the frantic rush he'd been feeling toward dinner.

"Sounds like you do have me worked out in your own mind, anyhow," Kiddo surmised. "And I appreciate being seen properly. Even by a spy," he smirked. "But now go hide in my room."

"I've just poured my heart out about you, and here you are, ashamed of me still," Dom gushed. But he loaded Kiddo up with the rest of the bags and started climbing the fire escape stairs. He took two at a time, and expertly avoided any near the top that had Jingle's sensors in them.

Shaking his head, Kiddo thunked up the internal stairs. He had to get started on that dinner.

Kid paused, scowling in thought as he noticed the stairway was getting pretty dusty. He'd have to remember that, or it would keep annoying him every afternoon.

It might be a good idea to take something for his headache first. But he really had to peel the vegetables and get them in the oven. The meat had to go in as soon as possible.

"Need a hand with those bags, baby cakes?" Sparks startled him with a spank as she passed him on her way down.

He blinked and reddened at the thought that she'd caught him just standing and staring. Head pulsing like an antenna transmitting radio waves.

"No, no," he managed. "I'm heading straight up to do dinner."

"Gotcha out of your freeze," she winked, and continued down.

She'd got his heart pulsing as much as his head, too.

| 10 |

Ten

"This looks delicious," Jingle chimed as she took her seat at the table. She splashed a generous serve of gravy over her meat.

"I'm missing the mash," Tiny grumbled, but was already tucking into his roast potato with no issue.

"I'm loving the cheese sauce Kiddo," Quicklips slapped Kid on the back, and Kid took his own seat between the burly man and the quieter Frazzle. He was feeling slightly successful.

"*I'm* confused as to why I had another detention alert from the school," Hato's voice cut across the table and into Kiddo then. "We agreed that you were going to do better."

Kiddo stared down at his plate, his eyes flicking over the peas and broccoli. Even grabbing the gravy had just started to feel like too much of an effort. He rubbed his brow in frustration.

Frazzle cleared his throat.

"Got anything to say?" Hato pushed.

Oh there was a lot on his to-do list in regards to things

to say. He should really tell them he'd become a mark for the snatchers. He should really bring up the fact that Dom wasn't a ghost, and that he could prove his own sanity by producing the physical evidence of Dom himself. He also needed to feed Duncan Jr, sweep the stairs, write a paper and put in an order.

But dinner didn't seem to have softened the one person who really needed softening, and for all the hyped-up energy he had, Kiddo just couldn't be bothered getting into it as Hato glared down the table at him.

"You had that test today," Sparks cut in to cover for his silence. She always remembered. "I bet you aced it."

Start pushed the gravy toward Kiddo, and he realised he'd been staring at it.

His leg was jumping, even though each jump was setting off his head.

"Let's work out where we're focusing tonight," Flip pushed his plate away and picked at his teeth with his dinner knife. "Get your plastic mat and magic markers out again Start."

"And I could show you all the stun grenade designs Jingle and I have been working on," Trix suggested, chewing a toothpick. "Sparks says they're really achievable to make."

Jingle quickly reached for her laptop to pull up the plans.

Tiny burped.

Quicklips and Hato were still watching Kiddo.

Seethe was up getting another beer from the fridge – pointing out that he'd written beer on the list and *somebody* had forgotten to get more. They would all have to pay for his mood because of it. But Kiddo hadn't remembered the list, the beer or his fake ID to get into the liquor store anyhow, which made it a triple failing.

Velvet had her high heels up on Jingle's lap, but her eyes were glued to her phone, ignoring the whole scene.

And Frazzle lifted his hand to Kiddo's forehead, pushing his fringe back.

"I think rest is need," Frazzle said. "Not want episode to start."

Kiddo glanced at all the dishes on the table, and then at Hato.

Hato gave a nod. "Go."

Kiddo pushed back from the table, loosening his tie as he climbed up the stairs.

That had been a disaster.

He mindlessly climbed all the way up to the library, and then out to the rooftop courtyard.

An absolute disaster.

Kiddo stared out at the orange skyline.

"Couldn't find the words?" Dom asked understandingly, hoisting himself up the last few steps.

Kiddo stared at him blankly.

"Listened from the kitchen industrial chute," Dom informed him unapologetically. "Hato really never used to be one to care so deeply. It's a good change." Dom sat beside Kiddo. "You good?"

"I'm fine."

Dom raised his unharmed eyebrow archly.

"Fine," Kiddo repeated for emphasis.

"You don't look so hot," Dom confided. Parts of his face were obscured by bursts of light in Kiddo's vision.

"I'm a ten," Kiddo told him.

"Well aside from that."

Dom shuffled out of his leather jacket and helped Kiddo into it. It was almost the right fit; just slightly too big. But the warmth from Dom's own body now passed comfortingly from where the collar pressed against Kiddo's neck and where the leather settled against his spine.

"Thanks," Kiddo told him, and was relieved when Dom put a hand on his own, stilling the drumming that Kiddo had been unconsciously beating out on his thigh.

"Frazzle told you to go to bed," Dom said then. "And you told me he knows his stuff. So let's go."

He took a firmer hold on Kiddo's hand and pulled him up.

"You're stealing half my bed again?" Kiddo asked. "It's the most use it's ever had."

"The least you can do," Dom told him, ushering him back down the stairs to the library. "Until you're ready to reveal me to the world."

Everyone was still eating or talking about grenade plans below. The clinks of plates and the sounds of voices carrying up told them it was safe to continue down to the bedroom level.

Dom very quietly closed Kiddo's door behind them, but turned to find Kiddo frustrated beyond measure, fumbling to un-do his already horribly uneven shirt buttons. His fingers were tingling too much to work.

"I feel constricted," Kiddo admitted, now yanking again at his tie, but getting nowhere.

Dom crossed to more patiently loosen and remove the tie, drawing it over Kiddo's head. Then Dom carefully unbuttoned the buttons from their random holes.

He grinned roguishly, crouching to quickly kiss the hard muscles of Kiddo's stomach before straightening back up.

"I told you, I like girls," Kiddo reprimanded. "That won't work on me." He paused. "Or, I thought I did and I thought it wouldn't."

"Sorry," Dom became business-like again. "Want a t-shirt? You feel constricted because you're clothed in the institutional garb of academic prison."

"Yeah, I guess," Kiddo managed. He hung Dom's jacket over the back of a chair, then stepped out of his shoes and pulled off his socks. When he straightened, he suddenly swayed and grabbed for his bookshelf to stop himself from falling.

"Woah," Dom cried, but didn't make it in time to help before Kiddo went down, and brought the shelf and its contents along with him.

"Cayden? Kiddo? What's happening?" Kiddo heard Dom's urgent voice, and felt him grab his hand, holding it as if he could keep him grounded amongst the chaos.

"Can't breathe," Kiddo panicked, as electric shocks seemed to rock their way through his body, making him twitch with tremors.

"You're ok," Dom said quickly, feeling his chest. "You're ok. Your heart is racing. You're definitely alive."

The tension in Kiddo's muscles made him cry out as if every single part of him was cramping, and he felt his whole body being wracked by convulsions.

The door banged open.

"What was that noise?" Hato boomed.

"*Dominic?!*" Seethe's voice hissed.

Someone bounced lightly over Kiddo, and cradled his head. It was Jingle.

Hato's heavy steps were followed by his savage expression as he stared at Kiddo's exposed chest and abdomen. The bursts of angry bruises covering Kiddo's sides.

"WHAT DID YOU DO?" Hato shouted, grabbing Dom by his shirtfront and throwing him with a crack against the plaster that had already suffered the loss of a bookshelf.

Dom was straight back up, palms out. "It's not what you think."

"NOT WHAT I THINK?" Hato roared, making to advance, while Dom sprang away from him lightly.

"You were ... dead." Seethe actually appeared as pale as Kiddo felt.

"Was not," Dom countered, putting the open window to his back. "Well, maybe for a minute."

"They turned you," Hato growled. "You've come back as a snatcher."

"Would a snatcher save a ten from getting snatched?" Dom put his hands on his hips, and then gave a pointed look at Kiddo.

"A ten?" Hato repeated, the colour now draining from his face too.

"I told you he's perfect bait," Velvet's voice carried in. "He's a ten. At the least."

"I can see it," Trix answered, nodding.

"No way, nine and a half."

That was Flip. He was fingering his switch blade. They were all filing in now, making a threatening semi-circle around Dom.

"They'll want him," Dom stated. "Brains, energy, looks. He also proved himself perfect gladiator material if nothing else pans out."

Hato's eyes went back to the bruises.

Kiddo had stilled now. This was the worst phase. He was turning rigid. When it really, truly felt like he couldn't breathe. Some part of him knew that consciousness would slip away soon.

"They beat to slow him. Not beat to kill," Frazzle affirmed. "Typical snatchers."

"Why was he even out there?" Hato rumbled angrily, the tendons pulsing in his neck.

Kiddo rasped.

"It's alright," grumpy Tiny was holding Kiddo's hand now. He'd slipped his way in while the others had all still blocked the doorway. "You're safe."

"He's out of meds," Flip surmised, peering at all of the popped bubbles in the tin foil packet left in Kiddo's drawer. "Must have made a drug store dash."

Quicklips cursed as he remembered the night before. "He did try to head out, but I thought he went to bed."

"When does he ever just meekly go to bed?" Sparks sighed.

"I'll head to the chemist," Velvet announced.

"Take Start and Quicklips," Hato ordered.

"Dom," Kiddo slurred agonisingly slowly as he used his last puff of air.

The others all blinked in surprise to find that the space near the window was now empty.

Kiddo's eyes rolled up. And he was out.

| 11 |

Eleven

"He's coming back around," Jingle's voice announced. "I hate when he looks like he's not breathing."

"He's still so pale," Trix stated. "You sure he's coming round?"

"Is good," Frazzle reassured. "Was only five minutes."

Kiddo moaned. It had felt like five hours.

"No second seizure," Frazzle went on. "Also is good."

Kiddo's head lolled as he felt the strong grip of Hato, he was sure, pulling him up and supporting him to the bed.

A hand cupped his cheek as his head hit the pillow. Sparks. Someone pulled up the covers.

"Should he still be this tired?" Trix.

"I remember he used to sleep for hours after a bad episode," Flip commented. It sounded like he drove the window down hard then, and locked it firmly.

Kiddo did feel exhausted.

Dom wouldn't be able to get back in.

"So, we have a ten on our hands," Tiny's voice stated gruffly.

"And we have Dom," Seethe said slowly. "Back from the dead."

Hato remained silent.

"We can't trust him to come into the fold," Flip answered. "After all that time, who knows what they did to him."

"He helped us," Jingle pointed out. "Or we wouldn't still have a Kiddo here to fuss over."

"Could've been trying to gain Kiddo's trust. And ours," Tiny rumbled. "Could be grooming the kid for a certain snatcher pathway. Or trying to get us all vulnerable for snatching."

"Most of us *are* close to tens," Flip asserted, blunt as ever. "And most of us are under twenty. Gladiator material. It would have been the motherload of all pay offs."

"We can't trust him," Hato sighed.

"But we *can* catch him," Seethe considered. "And maybe hear him out."

Their words circled in Kiddo's head for a moment, before he lost whatever grasp he'd had on wakefulness, and sank under the weight of his own fuzzy brain and depleted body's mass.

Then there were a few slivers of clarity, slotted between groggy blinks, and the heaviest of sleeps. As if his body was catching up on every sleepless hour he'd ever had.

"Pill delivery," Velvet's whisper woke him at one point. He could smell her musky perfume. "They're next to your bed."

He heard her set down a glass of water, and was surprised when she came closer to brush his hair back from his eyes and to pull his cover up again.

She seemed to circle over him. Rotating along with his dizzy mind.

A touch on his chest, as if someone was splaying their hand over his heart woke him next.

"Why don't you let us take care of you?" Sparks asked softly. "We care about you. I care about you."

Her hand stayed where it was, a comforting warmth and weight, as he sank back into the depths of nothing.

"I don't mean to push you so hard," Hato was saying the next time, when Kiddo became aware that Sparks' hand was missing from his chest.

Hato was staring out the window.

"You just have so much potential. And I want to keep it safe. Make it grow." Hato's hands bunched. "You need to be more careful. Then I won't worry about you."

"You ..." Kiddo mumbled, and Hato turned to him, as if surprised he was actually awake. "You don't worry as much," he swallowed thickly, "about the others."

"They are less worrisome," Hato replied in a low voice. "But I still worry for all of them for different reasons. I care for all of them."

Kiddo managed a lopsided half smile. "Dad."

Hato managed his own smile back.

| **12** |

Twelve

"It hurts," he groaned, waking himself up with the words.

"Mmm? Where?"

He started with a tense jolt, sitting up in a flash, and then giving another groan.

It was still dark and quiet in his room. But there was a weight on the bed beside him.

"Everywhere." His throat was dry.

There was shifting beside him. Two hands took hold of one of his and began massaging his palm.

He felt the tension drop from his shoulders, and he leaned back against the bedhead.

"Dom?"

"Yeah?"

"How're you in here?"

The massaging moved up to his forearm, and Kiddo hissed with both pain and gratitude as the tightness and strain were kneaded away.

"Cooling vent," Dom replied. "They don't just exist in the kitchen."

"Sneaky."

The massaging moved to his bicep now, working the muscle.

"I'm enjoying the Dom sized industrial chutes through this joint," Dom mused. "And you guys can in turn enjoy the free dusting service."

"Hato won't take kindly to you not being safely shut out of this room," Kiddo sighed, and winced as Dom's methodical hands moved to his shoulder and neck. He leaned forward obligingly.

"Surely Hato remembers that a locked window couldn't stop me. Or the snatchers, if they put their minds to it," Dom answered calmly. "Though I'd say the height of your room and the position of the fire escape would be putting them off the idea of abduction. It would be too messy and tricky. Falls would be bound to happen. Necks would be bound to be broken."

"So … you grooming me for the snatchers to get easier access?" Kiddo remembered Tiny's words.

"Pft." Dom's hands roamed to his other shoulder, and Kiddo angled forward, resting his head on his drawn-up knees.

"Look, I can understand what the gang are thinking," Dom replied properly after a moment. He pushed Kiddo forward and scooted behind him for better reach, hemming Kiddo in with long legs stretched out on either side of him. "I was thinking the same thing about Hato and Seethe, and spied on you all to get rid of my own suspicions. So, tell them I'll come to dinner tomorrow. And we'll talk it out." He dug his thumbs into the knots under Kiddo's shoulder blades so that Kiddo held his breath.

Kiddo realised that this was the most stillness he had exhibited in forever, and he hadn't popped either of his prescription meds yet.

"Also, I'm not grooming anyone, I can hardly groom myself," Dom added for good measure.

"As much as I'm glad to hear that," Kiddo murmured, in ecstasy. "And as much as I need what you're doing right down to my bones," he went on. "I don't much like the idea of Hato finding you in here. A fall would be bound to happen, and a neck would be bound to break."

"No fear." Dom's fingers traced the length of Kiddo's spine with a tickle, before circling outward over ribs and kidneys.

"None?"

"I had to sneak out once for Velvet. Twice when Sparks came to check on you. And once for the great Hato himself." Dom roved his hands back up toward Kiddo's other shoulder. "Or I guess I didn't sneak out as much as in. Back into the cooling. Your vent is conveniently located."

"Low in the wall, hidden on the other side of the bed," Kiddo realised.

"Yep."

"Sparks came twice?"

"You know, she really didn't mind that your shirt was off," Dom informed him. "It was lucky you felt so constricted earlier and made me get it off you."

Dom's jacket and Kiddo's school shirt were still hanging off the back of Kiddo's reading chair.

"How do you mean?"

"She couldn't keep her hands or eyes off you either," Dom answered with a smile in his voice. "I like her."

"You can't have her." Kiddo wasn't sure if he didn't want to share Sparks with Dom, or share Dom with Sparks.

"Is she yours?"

"She's her own."

"Are you hers?"

"I'm my own."

"Just like me," Dom answered. "A perfect trio." The breath from his words touched Kiddo's skin before Dom bit Kiddo's shoulder – not hard. But enough to make Kiddo's head come up and to make him suck his breath in.

"You taste salty," Dom announced.

Kiddo grimaced. "Having a seizure is hard work. I need to shower."

"Dusting industrial chutes is hard work. So do I."

"Now that's asking for trouble," Kiddo replied in a low voice.

"We'd get caught on the way to the bathrooms," Dom agreed.

"Yes. And also trouble because I already told you I like girls."

"Oh, and I listened," Dom agreed. "And wholeheartedly like them too. Love is love."

"You're not in love with me," Kiddo corrected. "Or Sparks," he said a little jealously.

"No fear," Dom soothed.

"None?" Kiddo asked warily.

"I don't need to seduce someone to be able to appreciate

and look out for them. For you. I hope for nothing but your friendship in return."

"Just friendship?" Kiddo asked, noting a slight drop in his stomach. "I'm not leading you on?"

"I might test the boundaries now and then," Dom admitted mischievously. "But I won't take more than you offer. And friendship is fine."

Kiddo frowned in thought, and felt himself relax back against Dom so that Dom stopped his massage, and wrapped his arms around Kiddo instead.

"In fact, I've long missed it. So friendship is *great.*"

Kiddo tilted his head backward to rest on Dom's shoulder. "No fear then," he agreed thoughtfully.

"So…" Dom said then, his arms settling like a seatbelt over Kiddo's chest and abdomen.

"So?"

"So the red, restricted access cross on your file," Dom began. "It's not just ADHD?"

Kiddo sighed. "Epilepsy."

He tapped-out of Dom's hold for a moment, and reached for where Velvet had left his meds on the bedside table. He popped the pills and downed half the glass of water in three gulps.

He passed the other half of the glass to Dom, who drained it, before they settled back as they'd been.

"Is that what keeps you from sleeping?" Dom questioned curiously after a while.

Kiddo scowled at himself darkly. "The medications can effect sleep. But *I* keep me from sleeping the most." He fidgeted with a zip on one of Dom's trouser pockets. "I made it a force of habit."

"Not a great habit," Dom observed. "Worth breaking. Although," he mused. "While for once it's not a school night, you've just had the most sleep I've ever seen you achieve."

Kiddo felt momentarily relieved as he remembered it was Friday – or Saturday now. His alarm would not be going off in a couple of hours.

"I, on the other hand, sleep well in any environment," Dom bragged. "Chutes, rooftop gardens, caves, a warzone, the bus," he listed on his fingers, which he tapped against Kiddo's skin. "I could teach you."

"I'm just getting used to your forced sleep techniques," Kiddo answered. "Now I know I can sleep on a work bench."

"You're welcome," Dom snickered. "But why did you get yourself into the insomnia habit anyway?"

Kiddo was slowly drawing the pocket zip open and closed against Dom's thigh.

"I always had most of my fits when I slept," Kiddo explained. "Like it happened when my body let its guard down. Nocturnal epilepsy. So, I dreaded sleep."

"Don't seizures happen when you're sleep deprived too, though?" Dom asked. He didn't seem to mind that Kiddo was rapping the fingertips of his other hand on Dom's forearm, which was still wrapped across Kiddo.

"Would that count for ironic?" Kiddo questioned wryly.

"Did your foster families try to get you treated and get it under control?"

Kiddo shrugged. "I didn't want their help. The epilepsy was the least of their worries in terms of trying to get things under control for me. I spent more time on the streets as a runaway than under any foster home's roof even before I was officially a street kid."

"Didn't fit with them?" Dom asked sympathetically.

"Did not at all. And it was all my own fault, all in my own head," Kiddo admitted. "I was a dumb kid, making shocking choices because I just couldn't accept a system relegated family as being real or right. I was enough to turn anyone off having kids themselves. And most of the families weren't even bad. They tried."

"You turned out alright in the end," Dom offered.

"I was feral then though. When the final runaway effort stuck, I let loose, burning all this energy – and more back then, off with alcohol, drugs, parties."

"You were eleven when you hit the streets properly?"

"Yup."

"And how did all that go?"

Kiddo shook his head against Dom's shoulder. "I stayed awake, because to sleep was to be vulnerable. I couldn't party in the clubs – too many flashing lights, and way too much of a young face. But I took my own personal party to the streets. I did anything under the sun and under cloak of darkness to get my hands on the substances it took to fuel me on. And I mean I did anything."

"I get it," Dom said softly.

"When Hato and the gang at that time – Seethe, Tiny, Flip and Jingle, found me, I was half out of my mind. Hyper, drugged up, beaten black and blue, and getting beaten further by a group of high guys who hated that a thirteen-year-old had beaten their champ in the ring." Kiddo grimaced. "I don't think they'd expected a kid to pack such a punch. But my winnings were life and death for me back then."

"Lucky you still have all your teeth," Dom said.

"Lucky to be alive at all, and not wracked with STDs or brain dead," Kiddo added. "But Hato decided to bring me up himself. To raise me up by a handful of my hair if he had to. A twenty-year old father, a club owner, and a survivor in his own right."

"You admire him."

"Course," Kiddo answered, only a little begrudgingly. "I needed his tough love. And I resentfully accepted it from him and the gang because of their own natures and experiences too."

It was odd to think back on it all. Four years ago, they had all seemed so harsh and hard to please. Especially Hato and Seethe. They'd all seemed so capable and mature already too – with Flip so well-travelled, Tiny a chain smoking machine, and Jingle already honing her dark web skills.

He'd hardly thought of it with any retrospection since. But, really, they had all been kids themselves, trying to raise a younger and worse kid. Flip, Tiny and Jingle had each only been fifteen.

"The seizures were bad back then, and my care for education and my future was zero. No school could hold me. Or stand me. Until the gang forced me to detox. Got me into routines and helped me work myself out medically. I started to feel less like an animal, and started to want to be better."

"I can hardly reconcile the person in your story to the person you are right now," Dom assured him.

"I've only been expelled once since then. With that head flushing incident when I let loose on the bullies."

"When did the others come along to the gang?" Dom asked curiously.

"Sparks found us a year later. She had a bag packed and was so business-like. As if she was applying for a job," Kiddo remembered with a slight smile. "Which in her mind she was. She was already a natural with mechanics, and could do a lot for Hato in that regard. And she was always happy for me to tag along and watch her work." Kiddo zipped Dom's pocket again. "As we got closer, she softened me up. She's just a year older than I am."

"Eighteen," Dom nodded. "Like me."

"Start came not long after. He was seventeen then. He'd done five years in juvie after leading a brilliant bank heist, but the adults he'd been working with were pinned as the masterminds and sentenced to jail time. The system didn't believe that a kid could have planned and succeeded to such a scale. They'd only been caught because of the suspiciously lavish lifestyles some of the adults of Start's team had suddenly developed afterwards."

"Not so clever on their part, but pretty impressive on Start's," Dom pondered. "Perhaps I underestimated that one. I should take a closer look at his laminated map and its scribblings."

"We've also had plenty of Hato's friends visit," Kiddo considered. "Trusted non-members who come and go. That's how we knew Quicklips, who has only stayed on permanently this year. He can't go back home to Mexico for a while."

"Oh?" Dom encouraged with interest.

"Caught kissing the daughter of a cartel boss," Kiddo informed him. "A lady who was already married to another allied cartel's boss."

"Ohh."

"And Velvet came with her elder brother from where they'd taken refuge in Europe a couple of years back. Her brother, Seethe and Hato had been sold to the same outfit of snatcher buyers, and escaped together. He used to bring Velvet with him to visit all the time, and he would teach me to cook."

"Where's he now?" Dom asked with a hint of concern.

"Marko. He was hurt too badly trying to break up a snatcher gang going after some kids from The Lair one night. We didn't have Frazzle back then."

Dom pressed his arms around Kiddo in a slight squeeze of empathy.

"Hato invited Velvet to stay, because she had no one else. And I kept up the cooking more regularly, because I felt like it was something I could achieve and be responsible for. It drew the others to the table and into a sort of family time."

"Flip appears to be more of a wildcard," Dom mused. "I know he's originally from Belfast, but it sounds like he's stuck around here for a while."

"Flip taught me to shoot and stab," Kiddo admitted. "Which sums him up. He does like to keep moving around the world. But he always ends up keeping an eye on what snatchers are doing in different places, giving us a head's up on what might filter down to us, and then ultimately coming back here. He was away searching for someone who might be able to help with the snatchers until recently."

"How did Trix come into it?" Dom asked then, smoothing his hand over Kiddo's taut sternum and stomach, and making Kiddo's own fidgeting pause for a moment.

"Trix and Frazzle were a package deal," Kiddo answered after a few heartbeats. "They're the most recent additions."

"That's an unlikely pairing," Dom commented.

Kiddo took a steadying breath. "Frazzle had just migrated here from Gaza with a head full of PTSD. He's a medic, and the eldest but most reserved of us. Seethe and Hato found him in the middle of saving Trix's life from a bungled snatch. She was hurt pretty seriously and suffered heavy blood loss."

"The snatchers had dumped her?"

"Fled when they thought she wouldn't make it to get their money's worth," Kiddo affirmed. "She'd fought back, but had fallen through a glass window and out onto the street in the scramble. She was left unconscious and with enough shard piercings to look like a glass porcupine."

Dom whistled faintly between his teeth.

"Frazzle had heard the crash while on a walk with his own night time demons. He was first to the scene, and was staunching the worst wound in her thigh when Seethe and Hato passed by on their bikes. Hato paid for her medical bills, and she's been loyal to the gang ever since. Frazzle has stuck around too, seeing people he thought were worth patching up."

Dom was quiet for a moment, but traced his fingers over Kiddo's chest again.

"I totally expected something like the gaudy club scene

from Seethe and Hato," he said finally. "I also completely got how someone as sure and steady as Hato could gather a gang of skilled youths to follow him. But I really did not expect him to be doing it all out of some kind of paternal care, and everyone to be sticking around out of mutual respect."

Kiddo stretched his legs out. "Even the club is an interesting story. One that doesn't reflect poorly on Hato either. But maybe you could ask him about that yourself when you close that rift between you. Now that you're alive again and all."

Dom nodded. "I'm glad The Lair isn't literally his evil lair for drawing in young people to be snatched. I was almost convinced that was what the snatchers had set him up to do."

"Talk to him over dinner like you said," Kiddo replied. He sat up and swivelled to face Dom. "I'll head out for a shower now, and then go down to get breakfast started. I'll tell them that you're coming so they have plenty of time to adjust to the idea."

Dom grinned. "I can guarantee it will just give them thinking time to work out which chair to tie me to."

"At least it'll be a kitchen chair," Kiddo offered, not kidding himself with ideas that they would welcome Dom in with open arms. "Your main worry would be if it was a chair on a lower level or the rooftop. And if Seethe or Flip was standing in front of it."

"I can't wait," Dom smiled. "This all sounds so nice. I'll bring them a bottle of wine. Or flowers, seeing as you don't drink."

Thirteen

Kiddo had never seen veins stand out quite so far in someone's hand and forearm before.

But the veins in Hato's hand and forearm appeared set to burst.

Kiddo had also never seen somebody manage to look quite so petulant or antagonising while their throat was being squeezed by such an angry hand.

But Dom seemed the poster child for haughty glares as he dangled up against the pantry door.

His boots were a few centimetres from the floor, and his bunch of flowers were a fainted pile below him, but he had somehow managed to fold his arms.

For once Kiddo was frozen, watching the scene in horror.

"Hato." It was Seethe who spoke, lazily rolling the word out. "You know he could have broken out of your hold if he'd wanted to fight you."

"He's been sneaking around here, working out our strengths and weaknesses," Hato rumbled. "We don't have to guess how helpful that would be to the snatchers."

"He's turning purple," Velvet observed.

Dom hadn't even finished stepping into the kitchen on the living level before hurricane Hato had hit.

"Kiddo set out such a nice dinner," Sparks added. "Which is getting cold. We might as well act civilised."

"And if we don't like what he has to say," Flip played with his switch blade casually as he eyed Dom. "We'll shut him up then."

Hato gritted his teeth, his jaw stiff. Before there was the sound of Dom's leather jacket dragging back down the pantry door and his boots touched down.

Hato grabbed the back of Dom's neck then instead, and forced him across to be seated at the end of the table where Flip and Quicklips sat close on either side of him.

"Water?" Kiddo managed weakly, quickly pouring some from the jug and passing it across Quicklips' place, which was between Kiddo and Dom.

Dom winked at Kiddo. Unruffled, if breathless. And still imprinted with the lines of where Hato's fingers had been around his neck.

"What a nice place you have," Dom husked at last, smiling around at all of the suspicious or dark expressions turned toward him. "Do much snatching from the club?"

Now Kiddo knew that was just to be insulting. Dom had already decided they didn't do that.

Hato growled. "We'll ask the questions."

Dom spread his hands out magnanimously. "Go ahead."

"Where have you *been*?" Seethe asked in a low voice then,

arms crossed and leaning back from the table already, though he'd hardly touched his food.

Dom speared a baby carrot. "Broad question," he commented, waving his fork and carrot with a frown. "Where to start …"

"The last we saw of you," Seethe pushed on, "you were being tossed into the back of a van that disappeared down the back streets."

"That's right," Dom's face darkened slowly. "If you want to go way back. I've been in a van." He ate the carrot.

"Where else have you been?" Tiny demanded. "Why did you let your friends think you were dead?"

Dom sliced into his neatly layered square of lasagne then, examining and then relishing the cheesy bechamel sauce that Kiddo had worked hard on.

"Good job," Dom told Kid. He was the only one eating. "If we stick to the van for a minute," he went on, "that of course leads us to the next place." He sprinkled some salt on his vegetables, swallowing the mouthful of lasagne.

"I remember the van pretty well," he admitted. "Because a trip like that sticks with a conscious, kidnapped eight year old who is fearing for his life."

Hato had a grey hue to his still unforgiving face.

"They had zip tied me, of course," Dom went on cheerily. "But I'd been taught by the best," his eyes went to Hato and to Seethe. "I broke and tore up my little youthful wrist in the process, but also broke the clasp."

"They wouldn't have liked that," Sparks commented. She decided to start eating too, and buttered a bread roll. "It would have knocked you down a couple of points in functionality. Costing them millions in sales."

"No siree, they did not take kindly to it," Dom agreed conversationally. "They drove me right out to the docks, and I thought I'd be sleeping with the fishes in no time. But here comes the next place I've been, where I'm sure Hato and Seethe went too, when they were taken."

"They guessed they went to a secret den at the cargo section of the docks," Start surmised. "We've never been able to pin point it on the maps."

"Correct. There are no windows wherever they take you. It's not easy to get your bearings in the cells, examinations or sales rooms. But that's where they assess, process and auction their live goods." Dom took another mouthful of his lasagne, and Kiddo noticed that a few of the others had begun to begrudgingly eat too.

"And what area were you sold into?" Flip asked with a hard glint in his eye.

"Clearly not organ donation," Velvet quipped. "You look intact. And alive, despite contrary beliefs."

"I was a hand me down," Dom answered. "I started off going for big bucks – sold into a European, behind closed doors, experimental pharmaceuticals industry." He scowled. "That did wonders in rushing puberty along by nine years old. But I was lucky enough to be pumped full of bone density increasing chemicals, as they used my wrist and a few additional, forced breaks to their advantage for testing. Turns out those drugs gave me particularly strong bones, even in my neck. They trialled a whole heap of sleep techniques involving the neck that a bunch of others never made it through. I learnt a great deal about that area."

"So we won't break your neck then," Flip commented. "Hato will go back to strangling you if you get out of hand. Or I'll stab somewhere soft."

Dom gave him a charming, wide smile.

"I heard that the pharmaceutical buyers do terrible things to those snatched kids in the name of curing cancers," Jingle uttered unhappily. She was hugging her laptop to her chest like a shield.

"Mmm," Dom actually put his cutlery down. "Kids who don't already have cancers to cure. And who can't reject inhumane methods." He coughed. "Anyway, there were a few too many incidents with swiped scalpels, impromptu acid bombs, and my own efforts to play with chemists' necks for them to want to keep me, and I was still too young and healthy to just dispose of. So I was handed down for a new sale to the cigarette sweat shop industry in South America, and then for mining in Asia."

"What happened there?" Quicklips asked, invested in what Dom was saying now despite himself.

"There were a few too many more neck incidents, or incidents of managers getting electric shocks or heads caught in machines and rockslides," Dom sighed. "I even escaped a couple of times. But they could track me down and back I went. Still too young and valuable to kill, and too annoying to keep at eleven years old, until they finally decided I would be the perfect level of creative for a different kind of sweat shop." He dabbed his mouth with a napkin. "Making weapons for a terrorist organisation."

Dom pushed back to relax in his chair, and Flip didn't even flicker with threatening bravado at the movement away from his reach. He was listening with a frown.

"I'd come with a sort of product warning, which meant I was specially chained to my bench so that I couldn't risk any accidents without risking myself," Dom stretched. "I was probably on the verge of gangrene from the cuff around my ankle, and had worked there for a couple of years before I decided to die."

"We heard you were blown up in an accident," Seethe stated flatly.

"I'm delighted you asked around about me," Dom replied rosily. "But it was no accident."

"How did you do it?" Hato asked quietly, his expression still impartial.

"Suicide vest," Dom answered coolly. "The other kid in the cell with me accidently cut his finger. They'd had that kid working with some crazy stuff, and the toxin he was working with at that moment got into the wound. He died almost instantly."

"You took your chance," Start supposed.

"Of course." The false joy of the moment seemed to have faded for Dom. "I strapped that kid into the vest I'd been working on. I grabbed a paralytic he had been experimenting with. I flipped my desk and yowled that the kid had swiped a vest from my workbench, and that he was threatening to end it all."

"Did they come running?" Jingle asked uncertainly.

"I heard them run the other way," Dom shrugged. "Better for them to lose two of us in a contained cave cell blast, than to get hurt themselves. But it meant they didn't see me take the paralytic, toss the vial, and bunker down before pressing the button for the boom."

Dom shook his head in memory.

"I was paralysed into the image of death. My heart and breathing slowed dramatically despite the adrenaline. Sometimes I felt that the gaps between each beat and each breath were so great that I really was dead during each pause. But I was aware of every single thing.

"I heard the roaring. I felt the impossible swell of heat. The surge of air. I felt myself and the workbench lift and surge backward into the wall. Something scorched my back. I hit the rocks like a rag doll. The sounds of shrapnel pinging against the cave rocks, and ringing in my ears.

"I still couldn't hear them, and was dazed, when they came in to scrape our remains out for the next workers to fill our spots. Paralysed, crumpled, bleeding, apparently not breathing, eyes open – they assumed I was dead, and threw me out into the desert to dry up and blow away."

"Lucky they didn't give you a proper burial," Trix commented.

Dom grimaced. "And also lucky that the dust packed itself into me and stopped me from bleeding out from a few shrapnel holes. I felt every burn and chasm on my body for hours under that sun, until movement came back to my body."

"Then you got out," Tiny stated. He was smoking now, his plate empty in front of him.

"No," Dom negated. "I was in the middle of a foreign desert, a warzone, and was more on the side of dead than alive. I got back in."

"Back in?" Seethe asked warily.

"They had everything a mostly dead person could need," Dom explained. "And I had their total lack of suspicion on my side. Back in I went, and worked on my sneaking skills." He smiled wolfishly then. "Which you all know are superb now."

"You go find the medical supply?" Frazzle asked quietly.

"Yes, my friend," Dom answered. "I got myself through. Even managed to plyer out some nails and glass that had hit me in the chest, and to find antibiotics for my ankle and burns. I was in a bad state, but I sure had strong bones, and a great immune system from whatever I'd been fed in the labs. I was also angry and spiteful enough to make sure I stayed dead only in name. Sheer will and a whole heap of good drugs from their stores kept me going."

Kiddo's eyes went to the welt-like scar twisting like a spurt of flame behind Dom's ear. It ran into the beginnings of a tattoo that continued beyond Dom's collar. The scar was a burn.

"And I hid, and recovered," Dom said. "Until I was ready for some payback."

"What did you do?" Quicklips asked.

A proper, genuine smile lifted the corners of Dom's lips. "I became their personal poltergeist. The happiest little trick-ster in a cave system of child-slaver, extremist soldiers." He took up the glass of water Kiddo had given him, and began to trace lines into the condensation on the glass. "I turned their chemicals against them. Random explosions became com-mon place. Slave kids kept getting loose and rebelling. Cut-ting throats. Then one night I rigged the place up with enough explosives to bring the caves down, and gave an evacuation warning."

"You warned them?" Jingle frowned.

"Oh, it was night, and they all found themselves somehow locked up in their quarters. Most of them anyway," Dom told her. "The evacuation warning was for the fifty odd slave kids, who all found themselves somehow not locked up. I herded them to the army convoys, and anyone who had a clue about vehicles got everyone else loaded up and we were gunning out of there before anything could blow.

"We pulled over to watch the night light up together. And that's where I got given my nickname by the others." Dom grinned impishly. "Raze. Because I 'razed' them all to hell."

"Well now, *I've* heard that name before," Flip cut in, his voice low but his eyes alert. He'd been searching for a person by that name before he'd come back from his most recent trip.

Kiddo saw Flip's gaze narrow in on the small lotus tattoo visible on Dom's forefinger.

"Back in Mexico an ex-snatched guy told me about how some devilish hell-raiser busted some of his buddies free from a desert sweatshop once," Quicklips added. "I didn't believe him. The story was second hand, and too wild. But it was similar to this one. And maybe the guy meant Raze, rather than 'hell-raiser'."

"What happened to all those other kids?" Tiny asked.

"Some came with me for a while. The drivers of each vehicle all took their chances with various well-worn roads across the desert, and ours led us to civilisation, which we could disappear into," Dom said. "But I'm not sure everyone's road was as fortunate. Chances are that, in the middle of a war territory, a car on the road will hit trouble. Chances also are that any kids dispersing into the city were still at risk from snatchers and starting the process again. I chose to move on, becoming a poltergeist anywhere in the world I heard of snatcher activity for the next few years. And I wound up in Japan for quite a while. Until very recently, of course."

"I heard that name in India," Flip announced firmly then. "And I heard it in Japan. You remember who I heard that name from, right?" Flip questioned Hato, who remained silent. However, Kiddo noticed Hato's eyes had flicked to the small lotus tattoo too.

"How do we know Dom here didn't just take someone else's nickname?" Velvet purred, twirling a loose, brunette curl around her fingers.

"Miss Lotus, who knows everything happening in the Japanese underground, described Raze as a man burning with the fires of a dragon, and rising to bloom with the grace of a lotus." Flip cocked an eyebrow at Dom. "She said he was the one person who had successfully gone up against snatcher groups, and even snatcher bases, time and again, and come out to tell the tale."

"Miss Lotus was infatuated with me," Dom flapped his hand deprecatingly. "She always talked me up, and called on me for tricky jobs. She took much joy in painstakingly turning my scars to works of art."

"Miss Lotus was renowned for her tattoo style," Flip asserted with a touch of satisfaction now. "She gave them out like badges of honour to the undesirables and rebels she loved most. She recommended I wait to see if Raze, her favourite, would come back to her den. She said he was the one to speak to if I really wanted help with any snatcher news or threats. She had no way to contact this Raze, but clearly adored him. And we were both disappointed when you didn't come back while I was there."

Flip had done quite the turn around. He sounded like he was already convinced that Dom *was* Raze.

"Oh, stop," Dom gushed. "She loved me. But I was in no way able to love anyone back at that point."

"She was seventy years old at that point, and missing teeth," Flip stated.

"That didn't help," Dom agreed. Then he rubbed his chin. "So, to answer your question, I've been in a van. I've been across a few continents, or under them, in their underbellies. I've been in Miss Lotus' den. I've been all over really."

Velvet pushed back from her chair. "The only way I can see that you'll totally prove yourself as an anti-snatcher ..." she began, advancing on Dom as if she were prowling.

"The ultimate, anti-snatcher," Flip cut in.

"Aside from Hato," Quicklips elaborated.

"Is for you ..." Velvet went on, stepping behind Dom's chair, "to get that jacket and shirt off."

Dom was unbothered, or, more like blank, Kiddo thought, as Quicklips took Dom's glass of water from him.

Dom coolly leaned forward to oblige Velvet, and she seemed to relish stripping his trademark leather from him, drawing it back so that it hung like discarded body armour from the chair.

The line endings of tattoo work were already visible beyond the sleeves and through the material of his fitted white t-shirt, as well as the one climbing the left side of his neck. But it was impossible to tell what bigger picture they were part of.

Dom stood for himself then, and turned his back to them all with a show of steely trust as he lifted the hem of his shirt up and over his head.

The first thing Kiddo noticed, was the absolute masterpiece of artistry across every spare inch of space on Dom's back, and presumably lower.

Blues, greens and black made up the background, with a mix of large and small lotuses seeming to float as if on water. Fallen pink blossom petals gave gentle splashes of colour, along with the dashes of orange, white and red as koi fish played around the lotuses and blossoms. But most notable of all, were the fierce, stark dragons bursting from the darkest shades of black.

Coming from the ferocious, snarling mouth of each dragon was a plume of burning fire that had not been tattooed there at all.

They were the mark of severe burns, that had been turned into displays of strength and a will to fight on.

They flared out from the soothing water colours of the background as if they still burned hotly on Dom's skin.

The most central and startling one seared across Dom's shoulder blade, down to the middle of his back, with the king of all dragons following it on his skin. Another burn, and another writhing dragon cut across his lower back and below the belt. There was the one behind his ear, and that dragon continued down to wrap around his arm.

Dom faced them again, revealing that the same patterns were inked across the left side of the top of his chest, running across his collarbone and around his nipple, over his ribs and wrapping around to join with the rest on his back. But the dragon on this side of his body was seated regally across his pectoral muscle, staring out with penetrating eyes. And that dragon's own proud breast was covered in silvery and purple lines that told of battle.

Shrapnel scars.

"So my early years as a lab rat actually bolstered my health," Dom remarked calmly at last. He pulled his t-shirt back on and down, taking his seat again and shrugging on his jacket. "Because I came back from some pretty bad things. I've lived a nasty life, keeping to myself, but I've made use of being alive by trying to keep other street kids alive and free too."

Kiddo was chewing his fingers, eyeing the others. But they were all still being surprisingly quiet.

"One thing I can reassure you of is that, I understand your reservations about me. I had the same concerns about you. Because we know that all of the people running the auctions, and those masked idiots doing the grunt work of harvesting youths from the streets, they were once snatched themselves. They were twisted into snatchers. And that's terrifying." Dom paused. "I can also assure you that they wouldn't want me in their ranks. In fact, I'm high on their kill list – when I go by the name of Raze. And I've come to warn that so are you, Hato. It's why I came back."

"What?" Seethe asked, finally husking a response.

Dom continued to watch Hato. "I heard word on the street … or whispers from all over really," he said. "That across the world a big fish called Hato was starting to rock too many boats. Usually what you do is an almost small-time inconvenience. Though every life saved is worth millions, there are plenty more being snatched every night all over the globe. But things are happening in your area right now that make your particular inconvenience intolerable. You have a target on your back."

Dom stood then, swiftly and unexpectedly.

He crossed to the pile of trampled flowers, scooping them up.

"I'm honestly tired now," he said, selecting one still reasonably intact daisy and pulling it free. "I haven't told anybody my full story, starting back at that blasted van. And reliving it wasn't that great."

He stepped over to Kiddo and set the daisy down on the table in front of him.

"Thanks for dinner," he told Kiddo, and dumped the rest of the flowers in the bin by the sink. "If it's alright, I'll come again tomorrow night, where more people than just myself can do the talking. And I'll tell you what I know or have figured out while you do the same."

He leaned against the stair banister for a moment, regarding Hato and Seethe with a genuinely deflated expression.

"I'll know if I'm welcome to stay by your greeting next time. But I won't bother hanging around to help, or leaving you unscathed in return, if it starts out like tonight," he warned, and made to turn. Then he paused again.

"Just one more thing before I go," he said slowly. "To answer Tiny's second question, about why I didn't come back, and tell you I was alive.

"An eight year old doesn't understand why his hero isn't there to save him. But an eighteen year old does. It was unfair of me to want you to cross oceans to get me back when you had your own problems," he told Hato. "I wished for you every night in my lab cage, hooked up to tubes or every time they set a bone. I wished for you every night in the factory, the damp stuffiness of the mine, the cave cell. Remembering you and Seethe ... that I'd had friends. It got me through. I couldn't come back and find out if you'd been turned into one of them, or find out you weren't a hero any more. I couldn't lose that golden part of before everything else in my life went dark. Even when I got out. I needed that image. Hearing your name spoken as a beacon against them, even a beacon that was about to be under fire, sounded too good to be true. And only the idea that you could still be that hero brought me home, to see for myself."

Hato looked stricken, and Seethe swallowed hard.

"See you tomorrow," Dom uttered. And before they could register it, he was gone – hand on the banister, descending quickly.

"Dom ..." Hato called, a little brokenly, after him.

Sparks patted Hato's hand, her face sad. "He needs a break. You'll get your second chance with him tomorrow."

Seethe scraped his chair back and grabbed three of the beers Kiddo had ensured would be in the fridge for tonight. They were all for himself.

"I'd sent him on an errand," Hato said in a quiet voice as the group regarded him. "He was so young, and Seethe and I looked out for him. But he was the tagalong little brother, and he was so tough. I didn't think twice about sending him to the convenience store."

"It was for gum and magazines," Seethe almost sneered at himself. He cursed under his breath. "I should have gone. I had the swiping skills."

"He took longer than he should have," Hato added. "It was just down the street. So we went to check. And there had been a fight, because he was so tough. There were battered magazines and a dropped stick of gum."

"And the van was speeding off, his little sneakers disappearing inside as they pulled the back doors closed and screeched away into the night," Seethe finished, swigging a great gulp down.

Jingle appeared ready to cry.

"You were both kids yourselves – just fourteen and fifteen. Then you were snatched in the same year," Quicklips recounted for them. "You weren't to blame, and you weren't left unharmed by what was happening on the streets either."

"No," Hato admitted. "But I should have known better, and protected him better." He sagged. "I thought that fierce little kid was dead."

| 14 |

Fourteen

"I thought you were never coming," Dom's drowsy voice came from Kiddo's bed when Kiddo finally climbed the stairs and crossed the corridor to his room.

"We had to talk about you some more," Kiddo replied, carefully closing the door behind himself.

Dom was actually in the bed this time, with the covers half drawn up. No shirt. Lying on his stomach as he hugged a pillow under his head.

The moonlight illuminated the designs on his back, especially shining on the tight skin of his burns, so that it seemed the dragons were spurting silver flames now.

"Did you just walk down those stairs, out the door and then straight back up the fire escape?" Kiddo questioned as he pulled off his shoes.

"Yep. Even had time for a quick shower while you all went on discussing," Dom answered with satisfaction.

"You smell like my aftershave," Kiddo noted dryly.

"Borrowed it."

Kiddo sat on the bed beside Dom, stretching his legs out

on the mattress and leaning against the bed head. Dom's eyes were closed.

"That must have been the hardest 'meet the family' dinner you've ever done," Kiddo joked. He wriggled a little to get comfortable. Then wriggled again.

"Mmm."

Dom's shoulder muscles were bunched and taut with his arms up under the pillow.

Kiddo couldn't help but reach out to trace the curving line of a koi fish's body. And then lightly touched his fingers to the rippled skin that had been burned. He ran his touch from Dom's shoulder, to the centre of his back.

Dom shivered, and Kiddo found that he liked that he'd caused it.

Kiddo traced the scar near Dom's hip and down his lower back then, and a lazy smile curled the side of Dom's mouth.

"Kiddo?" Dom asked in a drawl.

"Yeah?" Kiddo paused.

"You offering more than friendship?"

Kiddo frowned. "I don't know."

Dom freed an arm and reached up to grab Kiddo's shirt, tugging him to lie down. He flung his arm over Kiddo's chest.

"Then go to sleep."

"I know I don't want the neck thing," Kiddo stated hurriedly.

"I'll let you try to be peaceful by yourself," Dom yawned. "Do your best."

Kiddo shifted slightly. Then relaxed under the comforting weight of Dom's arm.

He stared up at the ceiling, willing each of his tense muscles to soften.

While he usually forced the letters and numbers escaping his brain to stiffen into line and into order, this time he forced himself to let go.

He sagged against the mattress, and turned his face to regard Dom's.

Dom was fast asleep, his light breaths making his arm shift slightly back and forth over Kiddo so that Kiddo didn't feel the need to move restlessly for himself.

He felt his own eyes close, and he was relieved to let them.

| 15 |

Fifteen

Kiddo started awake, stiffening as he often did. But then relaxed as he took in Dom … Raze … beside him.

Pieces of dark hair had fallen forward over Dom's forehead in loose flicks, and his brow was furrowed slightly, as if his dreams were serious affairs.

His tattooed arm was hooked up under the pillow beneath his head now, offering Kiddo a spectacular view of Miss Lotus' intricate skill on Dom's chest, ribs and biceps.

The greens melting into the blues of the lagoons on his skin. The blackness of the night sky canvas she had made of his chest. The ferocity of the mighty dragon curved around the side of his nipple.

Kiddo could see the glinting, hook-like nicks that would have been shrapnel tears, rent deeply open all those years ago. And other marks, some old and some new, that either wove seamlessly into the inked designs, or went beyond them.

One angry welt, long healed, but still painful looking, was visible from where the covers were draped over Dom's stomach. Kiddo couldn't help himself, and slowly, carefully pulled the covers down to see that both the tattoos and the ferocious wound extended down from the base of Dom's left rib, to below his hip and underwear line.

The tattoos appeared to trail away somewhere down the side of Dom's thigh.

Dom's forehead stitches were also healing well, but would leave their mark. Though every mark was beautiful on Dom.

Beautiful. Not intimidating, as this Raze aspect of Dom had the potential to be.

Kiddo considered all of this, until Dom cracked one eye open, and gave him a lopsided grin.

"Wishing you could come up with a polite way to ask me to stop using your bed?"

"You wouldn't be using this bed if I didn't approve," Kiddo told him straight. "Although maybe you're enjoying it less than the air conditioning chutes," he remarked. "You were frowning."

Dom's expression darkened slightly, as if a shadow had crossed his face. "Speaking so candidly of the past did not agree with me yesterday," he admitted. "I half hope Hato punches me in the face this time, so I can punch him back and skip the feelings with dinner."

"I'm making homemade dumplings, in case that helps," Kiddo offered. "A weekend treat."

Dom thought about it, and then nodded lethargically. "It does help."

He sat up then.

"But if I'm running late for dinner, I apologise. Please tell the others I mean to come, mainly because I'm promising you that I mean to come, but to go ahead without me."

Kiddo registered a slight drop of disappointment in his stomach that Dom was headed out somewhere else.

"Got big plans for today?" he asked casually.

Dom went to grab his shirt from the previous day, but Kiddo scooted up and selected a more comfortable, clean, light blue tee from his own wardrobe. One of his favourites.

Dom accepted it with delight.

"I'll take care of it," he promised, before answering Kiddo's question as he dressed. "I haven't been in these parts properly for a long time. I got to know the gang well across my nights here, but my days have been for exploring our surrounds and sussing out the situation. For my own peace of mind, I'm going to do some more wandering and learning."

Kiddo nodded, trying not to be flat. "You don't want company?"

"I would enjoy your company," Dom stated openly as he put on his jacket last. "But you need to write a paper, and keep your ten out of ten self off the streets. Even in daylight for now. Take someone like Flip, Trix or Quicklips if you need to pick up ingredients."

Dom lifted the window and sat himself half in, half out, his leg dangling on the other side.

"One of these days I'm going to fit a much better lock to your bedroom window and the fire escape door in the library. I'll show Jingle exactly where to install more sensors."

Kiddo snorted. "Just not yet."

"Not yet," Dom agreed, and then swung down to vault himself across to the fire escape stairs.

Kiddo was slightly deflated as soon as Dom's simultaneously larger than life and easy-going presence was gone from his room. He grabbed Dom's shirt and went down to the laundry level with it, running the material through his hands before adding it to the washing machine and starting a load.

He sighed. Feeding Duncan Jr, seeing if anyone was keen for breakfast, doing a general tidy-up, writing that paper, setting out dinner … he had plenty of things on his own to-do list today too.

| 16 |

Sixteen

"Don't pull at your hair so much," Sparks reprimanded him lightly.

Kiddo blinked, and quickly made an effort to untangle the mess he'd made.

"Now you're chewing your lip," she teased. "Don't worry so much."

She was peering at him from where she leaned over the open bonnet of Seethe's truck.

Kiddo's satchel and books were spread across one of her work benches close-by.

"Why do you think neither of them came to dinner?" Kiddo asked her, leaning on his barely touched essay – even though it was now at least ten o clock. He'd got distracted and this particular thing had slipped down on his to-do list.

She shrugged, pausing to wipe her cheek with the back of her hand – leaving an endearing mark behind as she did. "They are both very capable people. I'm sure they're fine. And it's their loss, because the dumplings were incredible."

"I put a couple of plates aside for them," Kiddo answered glumly.

For all of Sparks' outward confidence, he was certain that she and the others were at least a little concerned. It wasn't like Hato to go off without warning and miss dinner. And in Kiddo's short experience, it was unusual for Dom not to follow through with his plans. For both of them to be missing dinner was unsettling.

"Now you're bouncing your leg too much. Your handwriting's going to be too hard for the teacher to read," she scolded, but only gently.

He put his pen down once and for all. "The words aren't meshing tonight anyway," he told her, giving up. "I'll wait until a hyper-focus hits."

"And Seethe's system is totally blown," she admitted. "I'll need more than a night for this."

"He rides it too hard. Just like his bike," Kiddo said distractedly, shoving his things into his satchel.

"Just like Seethe in general," she agreed, closing the bonnet and wiping her hands on a cloth.

Seethe's c-gars, bikes and cars were always in need of the most maintenance above everybody's. But Sparks always took on any challenge he gave her.

Seethe had been the one to tell her about Hato and the work she could do as part of Hato's gang. He'd told her that her vehicles were always the best he'd ever stolen, and how she could make a proper profit, gain honest customers and make a life for herself if she left the gang she already worked for.

In a way, Kiddo had a lot to thank Seethe for on that front.

"Are you really going to be any better off without your essay to put your energy into?" Sparks asked then, noting how restless he already was.

"Want to punch each other?" he asked in return, crossing to the training equipment rack and grabbing some boxing gloves and a padded block.

"Well," she grinned. "Alright." She unbuttoned and rolled down her garage overalls, tying the sleeves at her waist so she wasn't constricted or hot.

He noticed with a skip in his stomach that she was only wearing a crop top underneath, so her flat midriff was exposed. He felt like he was made up of fizzy drink, and somebody had just dropped a Mentos right into his middle.

"You be the punching bag first," she told him, pulling her hand into a glove and then letting him help her into the second.

He was perhaps a little too slow settling the cuff around her wrist, pressing it there comfortably with overdone attentiveness.

"So, what do you think about Dominic?" she asked as she moved back and started to circle him slowly.

That threw him, and he nearly didn't lift his block in time as she jabbed a fist his way.

"Uh," Kiddo managed. "I like him."

"He seems to like you too," she said, and then cheekily ducked around him to try to punch him in the kidneys.

Kid scooted out of the way and caught the blows in quick succession against the shield. He cleared his throat. "I feel like he gets me," he answered at last.

"I get you too," she stated, almost jealously, Kiddo thought.

"Oh?" Kiddo raised an eyebrow, and his blocker again.

She was keeping him on his toes, all the while dancing lightly on her toes herself – rhythmically, as if she were unconsciously moving to the music thumping below, and they were in a dance.

"I mean," she said, and paused for a second, maybe to get her breath, or to collect her thoughts. "We all do."

She came at him with six fast jabs and a kick that sent him stepping backward with the force. But she danced closer.

"We call you Kiddo," she said, with her breath back now. "But it's not because you're the baby. You're the heart."

Kiddo smiled at her.

Cayden Lake had been a lost boy, living with abandon. Kiddo belonged to a family like hers, and he was trying to work himself out. Starting to learn habits and behaviours that helped a little, and finally discovering stability.

"Woah," he quickly refocused, and caught her boot against his shield again.

"I see you *very* clearly," she added with emphasis, grimacing with the effort she threw behind her next punch. She was trying to make him back up.

"And I appreciate it," he informed her. Doing his best not to budge.

"I guess Dom has good taste if he takes the time to see you clearly too," Sparks admitted then.

This time he was forced to step back with her blows, despite his best efforts.

"I like him," Kiddo repeated.

"I like him too," she confided.

He stepped back again. "Oh…?"

"He's –" she gave him a high kick. "Charismatic."

"Hmm."

"Fascinating," she added between punches.

"Sounds like you see him very clearly too," Kiddo was the one to have a jealous touch to his tone now.

He realised once again that he wasn't sure if he didn't want to share Sparks with Dom, or share Dom with Sparks. Or maybe it was both.

Either way, he was aware it was selfish.

She suddenly seized his shield and tossed it away, making him lift his palms to catch her fists as she started to punch his hands in time to the music – still bouncing from foot to foot.

"You like him then," she mused between breaths as she moved.

"You like him too," Kiddo answered wryly.

"Maybe," she granted. She was working up a mist of sweat so that some of the sharp edges of her short hair had started to cling to her neck.

She said nothing for a moment, and then stopped, with her knuckles pressed into his palms so that his hands automatically closed around hers.

"But do you like *me*?" she asked then.

Kiddo was taken aback.

Her dark eyes stayed on his face.

"I …" he spluttered with an awkward cough, feeling his face flush. "Yes."

She nodded thoughtfully, lowering her fists so that his hands followed. "Good."

"Where did ..." Kiddo tried to sort out his even more jittery than usual mind. "Where did this conversation come from?"

"To be honest," she mulled it over. "I've never seen someone like Dom before," she started, and Kid blanched.

"And, I've never seen *you* pay such attention to anyone before. I've never seen you with someone like *Dom* before. It makes me pay even greater attention myself."

Kiddo was flummoxed. He'd been waiting for her to say something like this for years – too dopey to do it himself. But now it felt almost like a betrayal to something else.

Sparks put her hand on his cheek as she often did, but this time she let it linger there rather than just patting his face tenderly.

"You're allowed to like more than one person," she told him, as if she'd read his mind. "None of us seem ready to settle down into a usual life right now." She shrugged. "But it turns out I don't really like that I used to be the only person you let your guard down with, and now I've discovered someone else is becoming that for you. I didn't even know you were struggling so badly a few days ago, but Dom was there to save you."

Kiddo frowned.

"You know about every test, you care about every restless night, you compliment every experimental meal," he told her. "You don't roll your eyes when I'm scrambled and forgetful."

"I spank you when I pass you standing like a stunned rabbit in the hall," she supplied.

"When I can't for the life of me choose between the ten things I needed to do, or remember the other five things," he grimaced. "But that makes for a much better jump start into action than Hato pursing his lips or Tiny steam rolling though me. You've been my constant, and you helped me through my darkest days."

"I think *you're* charismatic too," she smiled.

"And fascinating?"

"Mesmerising," she affirmed seriously. "Though for your sake I wish you weren't a ten."

He hooked a hand behind her neck so that the tips of her hair played across his skin. His other hand reached downward to pull her closer by the knotted sleeves of her overalls at her waist.

He was just leaning down toward her, his vision filled by her dark, eye-lined eyes, the grease smudge on her cheek, the quirk to her lips, when one of the roller doors out to the street started to rattle open.

It only opened slightly, before two fast figures half rolled, half skidded under, and the door rolled downward again.

"Give us a hand!" Hato ordered when he saw Kiddo and Sparks. He was already springing back up to his feet.

"Don't fuss," Dom glowered, waving him away as Hato hauled him up to his feet.

Dom was clutching his side, and though his jacket was covering his hand, Kiddo had a bad feeling. Even from there, Kiddo could see that the nice stitches in Dom's forehead also did not appear so neat anymore, as if he'd suffered another head trauma to the same spot.

"Get Frazzle," Hato told Sparks, and she was gone in moments.

Kiddo hurried across the distance to Dom, who had now stood himself apart from Hato. But Dom allowed Kiddo to come forward, and lift the leather jacket away from Dom's side.

Dom's hand was patchworked with red stains from where he was putting pressure over a wound. He was looking meaner than Kiddo had seen him look, apart from during the incident in the alley. Kiddo was hesitant, but glad to be accepted as he slipped under Dom's arm in support.

"Sorry about your t-shirt," Dom muttered in his ear. "And your dinner." He scowled at Hato. "Somebody complicated my plans."

Hato had crossed his arms, ready to retort angrily, until he saw Dom sway a little, even in Kiddo's hold.

Resolutely, and ignoring Dom's stare of daggers, Hato closed the gap between them, and the larger man stooped to take Dom's weight too. He ducked under Dom's free arm, and pressed his own strong hand into the wound in Dom's side, then guided the three of them across to the work bench that Kiddo had recently cleared of textbooks and notes.

"I saved you a plate," Kiddo reassured Dom, as he helped him to lean back. "And who cares about the t-shirt."

Dom circled his arm around Kiddo's neck so it was more like a loose hug. "Thanks. But I care. And I wanted to be there when you were serving them fresh." He turned much harder eyes and tone on Hato then. "Do you need to bolster the number of people guarding this place?"

"Seethe, Tiny, Quicklips and Jingle are all out there," Hato grunted. "Trix and Velvet are also heading out now for backup. The sensors were tripped, so they were moving to investigate already."

Kiddo had thought Hato and Dom were warming back up to, or at least feeling more understanding of each other after the night before, and opened his mouth to ask –

"What happened?" Flip's voice demanded, as he, Start, Frazzle and Sparks hurried down the stairs to the garage level.

Dom remained stoutly silent.

Hato cleared his throat.

Kiddo peered from one to the other.

Frazzle rushed forward with his medical bag. "Please, up," he gestured for Kiddo to lift Dom.

Kiddo quickly made to help lever Dom up onto the bench, and Dom eased back to lean on his elbows.

"He wouldn't let me take him to a hospital," Hato rumbled sourly.

"It's nothing," Dom shook his head. "And I'm not being a stoic idiot," he added flatly. "I literally know it's just a surface wound and it has barely bled. The guy had a flashy, clean knife. There are worse things."

Frazzle rolled the light blue, borrowed t-shirt up Dom's stomach to reveal a sluggishly bleeding gash that was a startling red addition, stretching from the right side of his naval to his hip. One part nicked the very edge of a koi fish tail flicking around his skin on his side.

"Is right," Frazzle affirmed Dom's statement. "Shallow, and not so risky. Not move too much and it start to knit."

Frazzle swiped a cloth over the wound a few times, catching a few slow drizzles of blood and cleaning the slice as he went.

"But head knock is worry," Frazzle reprimanded as he pressed a long adhesive bandage across Dom's stomach.

"See?" Hato scowled. "As I said."

Some of Kiddo's stitches had burst, though they had apparently done a good job in reinforcing Dom's skin, and the original cut hadn't reopened. Instead, the skin was purple and tight looking, with a new bruise already surfacing.

Frazzle decided to remove the now loosened suturing, picking the thread out and then wiping at Dom's forehead with a fresh cloth too.

"Risky. Second impact syndrome not good," Frazzle stated.

Dom held still, respectful and listening. "I'd got over any fatigue and headaches from the first head knock before this one happened," he told the medic. "I *was* dizzy and a bit blurry when we first crashed our way back in here, but that was probably breathlessness and adrenaline."

"You ring in ears?" Frazzle asked. "You sensitive of light?"

Dom shook his head gently. "And even my judgement and aggression levels are just as unstable as they usually are," he smiled.

Frazzle considered him, peering into Dom's blue eyes. Then he nodded. "Ok. We watch over. But I think ok."

Dom rolled the t-shirt back down, and sat up, ready to slip forward off the bench.

"No," Frazzle stopped him with a firm hand to his chest.

"Rest." The medic turned to Hato. "He needs the nice room to sleep."

Hato was surly, but he nodded. "We have a few spare."

"It's fine," Dom said. "I'll sleep here," he patted the bench. "I've seen others do it quite comfortably." He shot Kiddo a quick smirk.

"We *have* a room for you," Hato stated with emphasis. "If you want it." His eyes went down to the floor, and the usually unshakeable man scuffed his boot.

It seemed he was offering something more symbolic than a place to sleep for now, and Dom considered him closely.

"It's the least I can do for getting you in trouble tonight," Hato added in a dark mutter.

Kiddo and Sparks shared stunned glances. That was the closest either of them had ever heard Hato get to contrition.

"I guess we'll see how it goes," Dom accepted slowly. "Check how we fit. How the room fits."

"What made you both miss out on Kiddo's dumplings?" Sparks interjected then. "And get in this state in the first place?"

Dom shot Kiddo a guilty expression then.

"I was on my way back for dinner. Admittedly still late," Dom told them. "When I caught two snatchers hiding across the street, scoping out the fire escape."

Start gaped. "What did you do? They managed to get so close!"

"Did you go full Raze on them?" Flip had a wolfishly expectant expression.

"I listened," Dom shrugged. "I watched."

"What did you learn?" Sparks questioned warily.

"Not much," Dom answered with a flat expression. "They were whispering about searching the place. Finding an in. And an out." He rubbed his jaw and eyes. "They were contemplating how they might be able to get away quickly with a lean ten and a bulky Hato."

Kiddo felt himself pale, and Hato darted Kiddo a glance. Concern on his face.

"Did they mention any strategies? Places we could pin point and work on?" Start pushed.

"They had worked out the levels pretty accurately, and knew which one Kiddo's room is. They're less sure of Hato's, because it doesn't have a window," Dom stated. "But the only obvious way up is the fire escape, and you can't easily smuggle people back down heights like that. Especially if alarms would be triggered, if a tell-tale van has to be parked in wait, and if you've got a bunch of mean, keen-eyed youths circling on motorbikes watching for exactly that."

He grimaced as he straightened his spine, making his front sting.

"I can commend you all on what a fortress you've made this place in terms of deterring snatchers," he went on. "Snatchers like to hit quickly and disappear. But to do any damage here, you'd need someone as sneaky as me to do small scale stuff, which you would catch before too many of you were dead. Or you would need an outright attack, which isn't their style."

"What happened then?" Flip asked, less enthused by all he was hearing.

"They decided to make a break for it, and get a closer look

at exactly how hard the fire escape access is," Dom told him. "I watched them dart over and get halfway up, craning to peek into Kiddo's room, before I followed them to strike up a conversation."

"You what?" Flip was astounded. "What does a non-snatcher say to a snatcher?"

"Nothing," Dom smiled a little. "But that sounds like a riddle."

Hato harrumphed in annoyance.

"A non-snatcher will never be listened to," Dom explained, rolling his eyes. "And here's where Hato The Great comes in. Take it away," he motioned at the stony giant.

Everyone's eyes went to Hato, and he shifted uncomfortably.

"I saw Dom," Hato rumbled. "I saw two snatchers. And rather than letting them trip the alarm, or beating their heads in, I saw Dom follow them."

Sparks groaned. "You suspected him."

Dom lifted his hands in a 'what can you do' motion.

"I saw him pull out a balaclava with the fanged, bloody mouth emblem," Hato defended hotly. "He put it on and casually went to join them."

Dom again said nothing, but Kiddo remembered his words: a non-snatcher will never be listened to.

"Where did you get a snatcher mask?" Start asked with a furrowed brow.

Still silent, Dom eased forward and pulled a balaclava from his back pocket.

Kiddo shivered at the dark polyester material, with its slitted eyes and ferocious mouth.

He'd been confronted by human beings in that alley. But their behaviour, intent, and that mask had sure not made it feel like it.

Flip reached for the balaclava and held it up. There were dark stains that stood out in patches, even against the faded black colour of the cloth. Somebody wearing that mask had bled heavily from the front, back and top of the head, and it wasn't Dom.

Flip gingerly set it aside. That was enough said.

"What did you do then?" Sparks prompted Hato.

"I tried to listen, and to watch too," Hato sighed unhappily. Dom sniggered.

"I joined them as if I'd been sent along. I complained about being sent out on a risky 'job' like this. And they were telling me why it's worth it. Why Hato and any tens are so hot right now," Dom led Hato to go on, rolling his lotus tattooed pointer finger in a hurry-it-up circular motion.

"And Dom was telling them why it would be more worth it to focus on someone else," Hato admitted begrudgingly. "He was telling them that Raze was in town. And that got them ruffled."

"Why would you out yourself?" Flip guffawed.

"Thought it might make Kiddo's window, and Kiddo himself less of a priority," Dom confessed. "Though what I've learned does suggest otherwise. And, no fear, nobody knows I'm here now anyway."

Sparks was suspicious. "Why? What happened to those two?"

Dom raised his eyebrows at Hato in an unspoken invitation along the lines of 'do go on'.

"I'm not so light footed at sneaking," Hato said gruffly.

Start snorted.

"I'll say," Dom agreed whole heartedly. "I knew you were following me from the moment I crossed the street this morning."

Kiddo gaped at Hato.

"This was an all day thing?" Sparks asked. "I thought you said you spotted Dom and the snatchers tonight?"

Hato cleared his throat, but said nothing, and Dom finally decided to save him.

"It was an all day thing for me," Dom elaborated. "Hato couldn't keep up and refused to just admit that we both knew he was terrible at subtly tailing someone." He eyed Hato then, only slightly less coolly than before. "If you'd just asked to work together and tagged along, it would have been alright."

Hato's shoulders rose and fell with a sigh. "I didn't realise you'd picked up on my presence."

"Does a daisy know an elephant has trod on it?" Dom asked philosophically. "I didn't mind that you were following me in a show of continued distrust. If I hadn't done similar things, I would think this was a gang of psychos."

He tapped his fingers on the bench. "I remember the first time I laid eyes on Seethe when I tracked you lot down. On patrol. He'd caught a snatcher chasing down an under-ager who had left The Lair alone. He was beating the snatcher's head in until the mask collapsed inward, and so did what was under it." He jutted his chin back at the balaclava that had been set aside. "It's where I got that."

Kiddo winced.

"What I do mind is that you got us both sprung in the end," Dom finished. "That's not very helpful."

Hato took all of Dom's words stolidly now. Then gave a curt nod of recognition.

"In my anger, Dominic was one of them," he said calmly. "There were three snatchers outside Kiddo's window, as far as I could tell. I stopped sneaking, and stormed up those stairs like a bowling ball, radioing the gang loudly for backup."

"Oh dear," Sparks intoned.

"Kind of blew my cover and cut my info swapping short," Dom said wryly, "when I had to grab the two of them by their necks and yank them backward."

"They drew blades," Hato stated. "They also had the upper ground. Dom stopped one from stabbing me in the throat."

"I wasn't quite quick enough to skip back a step and miss the arc of his swing around," Dom pulled a face. "But I booted him over the side of the railing, and Hato clubbed the other one in a very final kind of way. Purely self-defence."

"Seethe narrowly missed being hit by Dom's falling snatcher, and the others pulled up, warning that they'd spotted a number of snatchers around. Watching and waiting, but slipping away when their patrols got close," Hato told everyone.

"They were probably waiting to hear what their scouts had to say," Dom mused. "But their scouts will instead be waiting for them at those seedy docks very soon, if Tiny and Quicklips managed in their clean up."

"We didn't really learn anything then," Flip commented, disappointed.

"Oh, I didn't learn a heap tonight," Dom countered. "But I had a whole day at it, and a number of other days before this."

"Where are you going then?" Start blinked in surprise as Dom slid forward off the bench and Kiddo quickly stepped to his side in case he needed steadying.

"I want those dumplings Kiddo set aside for us," Dom answered. "You best come too, or you'll miss out on your serve," he told Hato.

"But won't you tell us what's going on?" Start asked. "We need to plan."

"Over *dumplings*," Dom emphasised, as if it were obvious. He had already moved between cars and over the training space toward the stairs, with Kiddo close behind him. "I'll try not to speak with my mouth full," he promised, as if the idea of that was what had surprised them.

| **17** |

Seventeen

Kiddo had just finished nuking Hato's dish, and was putting it down in front of the big man, while Dom was already tucking into his.

"Absolutely divine," Dom complimented the chef, not phased by everyone's eyes on him.

Kiddo heard the blub of Duncan Jr. in his tank, and the intermittent beep of the dryer in the next room as it tried to signal to somebody that the load had long finished. Oops. He chewed his thumb knuckle distractedly, wondering if Dom was relishing the taste of the ginger and sesame in the dipping sauce, or if maybe it was too much.

But he pulled the scraps of his thoughts together when Dom beckoned with a tattooed finger and pointed at the seat beside him – motioning for Kiddo to come over.

Kid shook himself and made to sit next to Dom, and it was only when he was seated that Dom started telling the others what they'd been waiting to hear as Kiddo had done the serving.

"Right. I can tell you that they are specially collecting tens at the moment, because a once in a decade event is happening here in this city." Dom speared another dumpling and chewed before speaking again, as promised.

"There's a different focus each time one of these events is held, because it's like an expo for a privileged few which showcases that specific thing. Last time it was a showcase of the most successful, snatcher provided, experimental cases of youths. For instance, *I* could have been put up on show, because I'd been bought from the snatchers and became a model of highly successful bone density medication trials. But the kid in the tank next to me would not have been show worthy because she lost all of her bone density and became a brittle thing who broke with a sneeze."

Even Flip looked sick at that.

"The time before that was a gladiatorial type show. Epic and bloody. But this time the major focus is on rounding up the most aesthetically pleasing young slaves to have ever been snatched. And I mean the *most* aesthetically pleasing."

"A beauty pageant," Sparks stated with distaste.

"Even more horrifying and cut throat," Dom assured her. "The ruling snatchers from every city want their own ten out of ten to be the *true* ten out of ten, because they win the prestige of greatest success and greatest purity and strength of stock for the next decade. There can only be one true ten to win, so it is measured stringently." Dom chewed and swallowed again.

"As the hosts, there is a lot riding on your city's snatchers hosting this event safely and well," he went on. "They get to really go to market and show off all their wares, so to speak.

And they can prove themselves worthy of being top sellers. But, they of course crave the double glory of hosting *and* winning."

"What does the winner get?" Velvet's voice crackled over the radio. They were all listening in, and she sounded as angry as Kiddo felt nauseous.

"They get top buyers jostling for their stock. It's like buying a couture brand over a copy," Dom replied. "They get to triple their prices. They get to become the wealthiest outfit in all the lands."

He pushed his bowl away and gave Kiddo an appreciative wink.

"Which means your specific gang has three problems," Dom leaned an arm on the back of Kid's chair.

They heard Seethe swearing to himself as he foresaw what those problems were. Kiddo could imagine him, leaning against his bike to listen, looking like a wiry, foul mouthed shadow of the streets, to be avoided at all costs.

"Problem one," Dom announced, "is that you are about to face an influx of even more snatcher activity. You have the reigning snatchers sending out instructions to all underling snatchers in this area that they must hunt down the most elite, most scarce, most beautiful commodity to impress the top buyers. All of the ruling snatcher bosses from around the world, and their teams, have done the same thing and are coming here to do a presentation of their wares on the day."

Dom grimaced then. "Meanwhile Kiddo here is honestly the greatest ten I've ever seen. A total show stopper, and they will be wanting to collect him. Especially if they're still searching now – it means their other tens have been the expected level of perfect, rather than the knock it out of the ballpark, almost hurts to look at, extraordinary level. On top of that," he went on, "they want a smooth event. Which means that Hato is standing in the way of them harvesting a sure-thing, as well as from harvesting much else in this area."

"Hato keeps disrupting business," Trix's voice groaned over the speaker then.

"He runs a guarded honeypot of a club," Dom added. "You all work hard to create a guarded safe haven for youth that would otherwise be out and at risk. They spend their nights with you, all in one musical, flashing oasis of skimpy clothes and bouncing bodies. Like one giant tease and middle finger to snatchers. Those youth have you watching over them and watching out for un-masked snatchers scoping out the talent in the club, and those youth even have safer trips back to whatever place they call home, because you're watching the streets. Meanwhile, you knock off any snatchers you find."

Dom rubbed his eyes tiredly.

"Rest is need," Frazzle commented sombrely.

"Yes indeed," Dom agreed. He scooped up his dish and carried it to the sink, rinsing it instead of leaving it dirty in the trough. "But I do want to say that, as bad as all this sounds, I think it was worth travelling here to stand with you guys against this. You're really making things hard for an organisation that is normally too big for it to feel any waves at all." He set his dish into the rack to air. "And I think we can use each of these problems to our advantage."

He was met with disbelieving and confused expressions, and radio silence from the others.

"Promise," he added for good measure.

"We'll work it out," Hato grunted, scraping his chair back. "But for now, I'll show you to the room that can be yours."

Kiddo gave them a minute for the two of them to ascend the stairs together. He wanted them to talk.

The others seemed downcast and disheartened as he straightened the kitchen around them and was then reminded by the beeping again that he should fold the dry washing.

He was distracted at once by the sight of Dom's now fresh shirt at the top of the load, and he ascended the stairs to return it. But he paused when he heard Dom and Hato's voices coming from a spare room at the end of the hall.

"So ... Dominic," Hato was saying gruffly, in a way that Kiddo knew meant the big man felt awkward. "The main reason you're back ... is because the big boys are going to be in town?"

Kiddo inched forward to listen from his own doorway so that he could slip in if needed. He heard Dom settle the heavy leather of his jacket, maybe on a chair or on the end of the bed, and then he heard Dom's zipper.

He had no shame, that one. Brazenly stripping off in front of the very likely obviously uncomfortable Hato.

In fact, he was probably trying to test how much it would take to scare Hato off.

"I'm back because I see opportunity in all of this," Dom answered then.

Kiddo could imagine him pulling back the covers and getting into bed with an air of complete comfort, with Hato left towering oddly in a corner.

"Opportunity..."

"Like I told you, I came back with the hopes that you were actually this nuisance to the snatchers that I was hearing about, rather than a corrupt club owner with a collection of young people. I didn't realise exactly what was going on with the hyped-up activity in this area, but that's worth sticking around for too. In fact, if we work together and pool our knowledge with Start's theories, I'm certain we can cook up something that will really cause a stir."

"I see," Hato answered slowly. "Right. Good."

There was a sigh from Dom. He was softening.

"I really did hope that I would find people worth risking myself for," he added then. "When I find my kind of people, I try to keep them alive. And that's what I want to do for all of you." There was a pause. "It has been a very long time since I have truly had my own kind of people."

"I see," Hato said again. But his voice was touched with a tone of relief, and feeling.

"I respect what you have done," Dom told him. There was the sound of shuffling to get comfortable under sheets. "You've given your gang jobs or education, purpose, heck even a library and family dinners. Things I wish I could have had. Wholesome things." There was a thoughtful stop then. "Well, maybe the seedy nightclub's not so wholesome for an environment to grow up in. But I get it. I can see the money it would pull in, and the sheltered place to blow off steam that it would give to young people."

"I ... won the club, my freedom, and Seethe's freedom," Hato answered in a low voice then. "It was how we got out largely unscathed after only a few years. It's how we can afford to pay bills and eat. Along with the clients that Sparks' and Jingle's skill sets bring in."

There was quiet again for a second. "Well, I did not expect that," Dom admitted finally.

Hato cleared his throat. "Seethe and I weren't put through snatcher conditioning like you feared. We were kept together somehow, and spent three years in a drug den, chained at the necks."

"Nasty." Kiddo imagined the crinkle of sympathetic distaste wrinkling Dom's nose.

"They were scum," Hato agreed. "When we weren't needed in the lab, they would rile us up, torture us with hot pokers as if we were bulls in a ring, and try to make us fight. But they would inject us with anything that was slightly off and going down the drains first. Apparently, it made it funnier to watch. I copped a lot of steroids – bulking me up like a balloon ready to burst."

"I can imagine Seethe," Dom said, with a cringe touching his voice.

"They would push him to extremes with energisers. He was like a berserker," Hato affirmed. "It was going to kill him."

"How did you turn it around?" Dom asked curiously.

A floorboard creaked as Hato shifted his weight. "One day, when Seethe was burning out and at the same time winding up to the point of no return, I just shouted the first thing that came to my mind," he answered. "They were always talking about the great gladiators they were purchasing, and lamenting their short lives in the ring. And before I knew it, I was challenging their best warrior to battle. The words were along the lines of 'I bet our freedom that I can take on your top champion.' "

"It's always to the death," Dom breathed. "Did you know?"

"I had been boosted up into a hulk of muscle enough to try. We were headed that way anyway, and so was the poor oaf they put me in a ring with. Sooner or later."

"Sooner for the oaf, obviously," Dom responded.

"They were astounded," Hato confirmed with a flat voice. "They definitely regretted agreeing to what they thought was an impossible attempt for freedom, but they'd invited their friends, and didn't want to lose face."

"What a loss," Dom remarked. "They must have been realising they had missed quite the chance to make a buck by turning you into a gladiator. Instead they were losing what they'd spent on two slaves. Surely they didn't just let you walk out after one success though, no matter the agreement."

"They called foul," Hato told him. "Declared that I had to prove I could do it again."

"And again?"

"I can still see the desperate, vicious faces of the guys and girls they forced me up against. I had to be selfish and single minded then, but now, it haunts me." Hato's voice was so low Kiddo almost couldn't hear it.

"Finally," Hato went on. "One of our slavers' friends bet their own champion and the deed to one of their factory sites against me being able to win a final time."

"You couldn't have been in great shape," Dom reflected. "They must have been certain you'd fail."

"I had no choice but to win anyway," Hato answered. "This

time I could walk out with our lives, a property to my name, and the other gladiator's life intact."

"Which you did? And they *let* you?"

"They said they'd never been more entertained," Hato told him grimly. "That I'd had them on the edge of their seats, which was worth more than a few slaves or a dilapidated warehouse could be."

"Seethe left with Marko – Velvet's brother, slung over his shoulder, and I left with a deed rolled up in my hand. We also all left with guns pointed at our backs, and dumped unceremoniously from the windowless back of a van. So we never knew exactly where we'd come from. And we could never rain down retribution on our owners like you did."

"Jingle couldn't track the last owner of the deed?" Dom asked.

"Tracked it back to where some legitimate owner had lost the deed to an unknown, intimidating other party in a poker game," Hato answered. "That was the end of the trail."

"Maybe they'll be at this exhibition showcase," Dom said with a hint of evil.

"Maybe."

"That's the mark around your neck?" Dom asked then.

Kiddo recalled the faint scar, like a ringed choker, circling Hato's neck, and Seethe's too. The marks from the neck cuffs were hardly noticeable anymore, but they were still there.

"A memory of a time we were lucky to escape," Hato acknowledged.

"I'm glad you did," Dom replied. "Look at what the lives of

the others have become because you made it out and decided to care instead of hate. I admire that."

Dom yawned.

There was the shifting of weight again as Hato took a few steps to the door.

"Dominic," Hato began then.

"Yes, old friend?"

"I am offering you your own room here. Your own place," Hato said. "I am offering you your own people – a family. Because you inspired this."

Dom seemed to be stunned to silence.

"Losing you was what truly made me start to care."

Kiddo quickly stepped behind his still ajar door, scarcely breathing as Hato closed Dom's door over and backed out, slowly disappearing down the hall to the stairs.

Waiting a few counts in case anyone else was going to appear, Kiddo ghosted his way to Dom's new room and stepped silently inside – easing the door shut without a sound.

Even Dom hadn't heard him, and his eyes were closed under a furrowed brow.

But Kiddo rushed forward as he saw Dom start to throw an arm over his eyes to block out the world.

Kiddo caught Dom's wrist before it could land on the purple, heavily bruised skin over Dom's eyebrow and temple. And Dom's eyes flashed open to stare at Kiddo for a moment in surprise.

"Thanks," he smiled then. "That would have hurt."

He moved to reach forward for Kiddo's other hand, slipping the clean shirt through Kiddo's fingers and laying it out on the bed beside him.

"Congratulations on the official upgrade to your own bed," Kiddo told him, shifting on his feet.

Dom settled back again with a wince. "Maybe every now and then I'll still slither through the chutes for old time's sake," he mused.

"Legendary Raze, or Dom the chute sweep." Kiddo gingerly leant over Dom and reclaimed the shirt, taking it to the empty wardrobe to select a hanger for it.

"Would you sit down?" Dom yawned again. "You're hovering."

"I'll let you rest," Kiddo answered, coming back across to straighten the covers that Dom had already scrunched up.

Dom grabbed Kiddo's sleeve and quickly kicked the sheets again so that they slid down, ready for Kiddo to jump under. "Get in and we'll both sleep."

Kiddo eyed the bandage across Dom's stomach, struggling to rationalise a reason for staying. He realised he'd come to rely on Dom's presence.

"Your room isn't safe," Dom added. He yawned again. "Please hurry up."

Kiddo grinned, stripped off to his boxers, and added his weight to the mattress.

Dom threw an arm over him and pulled him closer.

"You good to sleep?" Dom questioned drowsily.

"I'm getting better at it every night," Kiddo admitted.

"It's a wonder what you can do when you try your best," Dom whispered – his words petering out.

But Kiddo knew it wasn't trying his hardest that was helping him most.

| 18 |

Eighteen

"Exactly how much time do we have before this place gets snatcher crazy and the expo happens?" Seethe was picking at his teeth with a knife, though Kiddo hadn't even started on breakfast for the crew yet.

Velvet was clutching a cup of coffee, looking dangerous after all night patrolling.

Dom was helping Kiddo fold the forgotten, rumpled washing from last night.

Tiny was attacking a stick of gum grumpily, as if the gum had offended him. He was trying to give up smoking again, after a club snatcher had apparently commented on the nicotine smell being a turn-off last night.

"The good news is, you don't have to wait long at all," Dom told everyone. "The bad news is, you don't have much time to prepare at all."

Quicklips groaned. "Two weeks? A month?"

"Try next weekend," Dom corrected him. "Saturday night. You'll be noticing plenty of big players and their stock arriving this week."

"No," Start uttered, aghast. "It's not enough planning time."

"Next weekend," Jingle repeated, astounded. Her hair had a clip-in extension that glittered fluoro pink.

"No fear." Dom smoothed a pair of Sparks' overalls over the top of his pile.

"None?" Kiddo said under his breath, getting a smile from Dom.

"How is there no fear?" Trix asked snippily. "Our local snatchers are going to be more stressed than ever about securing themselves our ten over here."

Dom held up a bra then, unsure how to deal with that.

Kid grabbed it and aligned the cups neatly to add them to the basket.

"Well, I studied Start's maps a few nights ago," Dom explained. "And," he eyed Start appreciatively, "you have picked up on a few patterns that have been very helpful in guiding my own explorations."

Start blushed, chuffed.

"Of course, you've all worked out that their base must be close to the docks, based on past experiences, their need to ship stock, their need for space and such," Dom went on. "But I did some chute shuffling through the warehouses in what you've identified to be the hot zone, and could find nothing particularly dodgy."

"This sounds like bad news," Flip commented, stopping himself from swigging from the orange juice bottle when he saw Hato looking.

"Or, it sounds like a process of elimination," Dom asserted.

"If a super wealthy, covert organisation isn't in plain sight along the docks, where might they be?"

"Is it possible?" the very clever Start had already caught on.

"It's the only thing left that I can think of," Dom shrugged. "There would be enough space. They would have the money to do it."

"It's the only possibility, the only angle we haven't considered," Start hurried to grab his laminated map to peer at it with new eyes.

Kiddo headed over to select the ingredients for French toast. This seemed like a conversation where food would help.

He was startled when Sparks quickly came over to join him.

"Teach me how?" she asked, and he nodded gratefully – catching a faint, completely non-jealous smile on Dom's face out of the corner of his eye.

"What exactly are you two talking about?" Seethe asked Dom and Start irritably.

Dom went on folding the clothes that Kiddo had half finished.

"I think they've created some kind of literal underground set up," Dom informed them all. "Under the warehouses. It would be so close to the water that transporting people onto ships would be easy to cover up."

"Wow," Trix commented, sitting back with raised eyebrows.

"Kiddo and I hid in a concrete pipe by the water's edge on the night that Kiddo was nearly snatched," Dom went on. "It made me think, how easy it could be to blend into the banks if you were hiding. How you don't actually need a pier to drop anchor. Maybe you could load a shipment, or unload live cargo through something else that would be almost invisible – blending in."

Hato was frowning in thought. "There are giant cement pipes that have been dumped on the water's edge for as long as I can remember. On the south side."

Start circled it triumphantly on the map in red marker. "They angle downward on one side, as if they've sunken into the muck of the banks."

"It could be more of a ramp," Flip speculated. "A pipe that big would have enough space for their vans to fit inside. A tight tunnel, but do-able."

"How would they access it, though?" Jingle crinkled her nose. "It's so muddy."

"The pipes have 'fallen' over an old unused strip of road," Hato negated. "It's a gravel trail that would intercept with the middle point of the pipes. If they swung out their vans a little, they could turn into an opening."

"It must be an opening that blends very well," Seethe said pensively. "Though I've never closely checked those pipes out. They've been there so long they blend into the landscape."

"I *have* noticed that the higher end of the pipes angle out over the water, and the banks drop down steeply there with the water getting very deep," Tiny rumbled around his gum. "An astute captain could manoeuvre in close."

"I could guess that the pipes might actually all be hollowed out into one cavernous tunnel, where traffic can quickly, unnoticeably flow in through the middle entry over the gravel. And stock can flow out through the end of the tunnel and into a ship. Though I am very aware that there are a lot of 'coulds' and 'maybes' in all this," Dom finished his folding. "So we need to do our research to confirm."

"What can we really even do if we do confirm?" Velvet questioned. "Snatchers are like ants. Everywhere. And we're just us."

"I blew up a terrorist den," Dom reminded her. "It wasn't easy or without pain. But one person has the ability to raze a whole organisation when they need to." He watched Sparks and Kiddo soaking a stack of bread, ready to put on the pan. Sparks was thoroughly enjoying the process.

"Raze isn't just *me* and my reputation," Dom went on. "Acts of rebellion from snatched kids or just from good people all over the world have been attributed to Raze, just because their activities align with my values and the rebels have gone unnamed. But imagine what we can achieve – an experienced and well-coordinated family, rather than one half dead boy. We would all be Raze in a war on snatchers."

"You want to blow them up?" Flip asked enthusiastically. "Rig the place up to blow?"

"It's one option," Dom granted. "Though we have to come up with a way that we can take out as many leaders and henchmen in the one place as possible, without making their snatched youths suffer."

"We'll never get them all," Trix said broodingly.

"But it would be the biggest blow the industry has ever suffered," Quicklips rubbed his hands together. "It would take them years to recover, and in the meantime, we could stamp out more of them while they're weak."

"Don't get ahead of yourself," Hato warned. "First we need to do that research. We don't even know if those pipes really are an entrance. And we definitely don't know what anything looks like down there. We don't know how they'll set up their displays of youth for judging – and we can't kill any trapped stock. We also have no idea how to get in and rig up whatever our method of taking out the snatchers might be."

"So we all head out tonight," Tiny rumbled. "Half do our usual rounds. Half watch and scout the docks."

There were murmurs of agreement, and then pleasure as Sparks and Kiddo began bringing over plates of toast.

"Except for Kiddo," Hato added stoutly. "Tomorrow's Monday, and you have a paper due."

| 19 |

Nineteen

Sparks came in and flopped on the couch beside him.

She and almost everybody who had gone to watch at the docks had come back after hours of inaction.

But, of course, not Hato and not Dom.

She sagged back against the arm of the couch, half asleep already.

"You been staring at that conclusion for an hour?" she asked. "Tapping your pen just like that?"

He sighed. "Yep. It's been finished since midnight. But my brain still decided just to stare at it blankly and offer up no improvements." He stuffed the whole paper into his satchel. At least she'd broken him out of that trap.

"Name on it?"

He grimaced, easing it back out, scrawling his full name on it, and stuffing it in again.

Kiddo's legs were bouncing, but he realised that she was just sitting there, trying not to go to sleep, because she didn't want him waiting alone.

"You take your meds?" she asked sleepily.

"Huh? Oh, uhuh."

"You feed Duncan Jr?"

"Yeah."

"You … ummm …" Sparks yawned. She was trying to draw his mind to the routines that often settled him when he couldn't unwind.

Achievable steps that he could tick off on a list usually made him feel like an at least somewhat sorted individual, rather than a forgetful scatterbrain, letting his thoughts whirl about like uncontrollable rings spinning around a planet.

He reached down and grabbed her legs, swivelling them up onto his lap so that her body followed.

"Now I'll fall asleep," she warned – finding herself nestled with the arm of the couch behind her back, and his arms cradling her legs.

"Good. It's fine," he told her. "Relax."

Kiddo unlaced her boots and dropped them to the floor.

"Lucky I showered." She settled back into the plush cushions.

He put pressure into the balls of her small feet, rubbing firmly. She was wearing little ankle socks with tiny hearts on them.

"Oh, thank my lucky stars," she sighed, her eyes closed.

Kiddo had often done this for her over the years – something he would have never done for any of the others, and something she would never have allowed any of the others to do for her.

He secretly thought she worked the hardest out of anybody, and worried that she might exhaust herself into being crushed by a car or something one day. So, while she hated leaving him awake by himself, he would do his best to help her unwind after big days fixing and maintaining the gang's normal as well as their patrol vehicles, along with the modification jobs of any other private clients who had discovered her brilliance. She also patrolled like the others on alternating night shifts, and remembered every single important or unimportant thing he ever told her.

He was satisfied when her little sounds of appreciation faded away with sleep, but blinked with surprise when Dom leaned on the back of the couch near her peaceful face.

"Hey," Dom said very softly. "Get that paper done?"

"Hey," Kiddo breathed back. "Find those snatchers?"

"Let's just say it was worth hanging around with our eyes peeled," Dom answered in a whisper. "We were right."

Kiddo shook his head in wonder.

After so long without a tangible location for the root of their problem, it had almost felt like the snatchers were hardly real. That they were wraiths of the night. Striking and disappearing.

But here they were, with a physical base. A human organisation. Worse for being human and evil rather than alien and evil.

"Did you see a way for us to get in?" Kiddo asked.

"We'll have to do some more sneaky scoping out with Start in the daylight while you're at school," Dom answered seriously. "But I'll fill you in on everything and we'll talk more about it all over dinner."

Kiddo nodded in appreciation. "Is Hato back too?"

"Wrapping things up at The Lair," Dom provided. "Don't you think she looks like a Greek Muse?"

Kiddo watched as Dom peered down at Sparks almost curiously, reaching for her and gently brushing her hair from her forehead with a light sweep of his fingertips.

"Careful," Kiddo cautioned. "You'll wake her."

"It never wakes you," Dom grinned back. "I think she's pretty wiped out. And you should be too." He straightened. "You coming?"

Kiddo peered at Sparks, not wanting to move or leave her.

"She won't mind waking if it's in your arms," Dom said persuasively. "I would do it, but who knows, my tiny gut cut could burst." He stooped to grab Sparks' boots instead.

Hesitating for just a second longer, Kiddo slipped out from underneath her.

"Just scoop her up with purpose. The more careful and halting you are, the less smooth it will be for her," Dom instructed.

As purposefully and efficiently as he could, Kiddo bent and wrapped his arms around and under her, lifting her easily.

Sparks murmured slightly, and rested her temple against his shoulder.

"I'll make sure you don't die on the steps," Dom whispered comfortingly.

Kiddo felt Dom put guiding hands on his shoulders, which he alternately moved to Sparks' head or small feet – acting as a cushion when they got up to her doorway and as Kiddo was easing her inside.

"Thanking my lucky stars again," she yawned as she blinked up at Dom cradling the back of her head, and at Kiddo carrying her toward her bed. "Thanks for the free trip."

"I speak for us both," Dom whispered as he set her boots down and pulled back the covers for Kiddo to settle her in. "When I say it is our pleasure."

Kiddo gaped when Dom swept close to press a kiss to her lips, and she laughed more wakefully.

"Good night kiss," Dom shrugged, straightening and stepping back from the bed. "You best do it too, or she won't sleep."

Kiddo was still gaping.

"You best do it too," Sparks reiterated.

And finally, he obligingly leaned down. One hand weighing down each side of her pillow as he stared into her caramel eyes for a moment, and then stole a slow kiss.

It was heated enough, with the soft cushion of her lower lip rubbing against his and her tongue flicking over his top lip, that he knew she was awake properly now.

"That was a wake-up kiss," Dom chided. "But we'll both do better next time," he promised Sparks as he gently tugged Kiddo's sleeve. "Because seeing that definitely made me want another one."

She had rolled onto her side to watch them retreat, and was grinning from ear to ear as Kiddo backed out of the room and Dom closed her door.

Kiddo hardly noticed being guided into Dom's own room again, because he was feeling jittery as hell.

"How am I going to sleep after *that*?" Kiddo almost crowed – but quietly – as he yanked his shirt over his head and started to bounce around the room, unable to find a perch to settle on. "That's been years in the making, and now I'm practically jumping out of my skin."

Dom shrugged, and crossed to him. "A goodnight kiss always works."

Without pause, Dom's lips were on Kiddo's, and his hand was on Kiddo's bare chest, over his heart, while the other pressed into his back.

Dom seemed to feel the tension gradually drop from Kiddo's shoulders as he relaxed and his heartbeat slowed under Dom's hand.

Kiddo himself hardly noticed as his own hands found Dom's hips, and shifted up his skin under his shirt.

Kiddo had become mellow, melted butter when Dom's lips left his – almost as if all of his bones had gone soft and he might sink down into a puddle.

"That stopped you," Dom observed, drawing Kiddo toward the bed. "Not one jolt or mindless fidget for a few seconds. Not counting the touching me up."

Had it only been a few seconds?

Kiddo was stumped and hazy as Dom threw the covers and his arm over him like usual, like a weighted blanket of comfort.

"You good?" Dom asked after a moment, muffled with his face half buried in pillow.

"Um ..." Kiddo managed. "Yeah."

"Sorry if I got carried away," Dom said quietly then. "Told you I like to test the boundaries. But I don't mean to test them too far."

Kiddo took a deep breath in, feeling the rightness of Dom's arm over him.

"No fear," he replied at last.

Dom's arm pressed him slightly.

"None?"

Kiddo considered it.

"Sparks told me," he began. "That it's alright to like two people."

"Well," Dom began. "I would say, for people living such offbeat lifestyles as ourselves, that she is completely right."

"Dom?" Kiddo asked.

"Mmm?"

Kiddo swallowed. "Are you offering more than friendship?"

"I'm offering the deepest kind of loyalty and friendship I've ever been able to offer," Dom answered seriously. "But remember, I don't need and probably *can't* even do a conventional relationship. What I do need, is *your* friendship. For you to be my person. And I will be everything you need in return. Whatever that might be."

Kiddo nodded, hearing his head move against the fabric pillowcase. "I think that is exactly what I needed to hear."

| **20** |

Twenty

"Morning ma'am."

The teacher did a double take as Kiddo slouched in on the bell, taking a seat on time, with his paper in hand, and without rumples.

It was only Dom's influence before the morning rush that had made it all possible, and Dom had borrowed a patrol bike to drop Kiddo off at school safely as well as ahead of time.

"Is your name on it?" the teacher asked, peering sternly over her glasses as she came to collect the paper.

He sat up straighter and pointed to the scrawl of his name on the back.

The teacher gave him an almost warm, if near imperceptible smile. She took his paper without further pause, and Kiddo spread himself out under the table in relief – feeling somewhat competent for once.

He hardly got called out for daydreaming during Science, for fidgeting in Math and for mixing everything up in History. Finishing up on sport was the perfect end to the day.

"You made running that field look easy," Dom complimented, waiting atop the gate pillar again as promised.

"Normally I get daily practice on the hustle to school," Kiddo answered dryly. It did wonders for his fitness, if not for his tardy record.

For once Kiddo was leaving with everybody else in a crowd, and a number of people were checking Dom out. But Dom had spotted and honed his attention in on Kiddo immediately.

He led the way to where a wasp-like patrol bike leaned on its stand, and Kiddo straddled it behind him, feeling the life rumble into it before Dom kicked the stand back and they launched away from the pavement.

Kiddo circled his arms around Dom, careful to hold higher than where the healing cut was, and soaking in the beautiful sting of heat from the surface of Dom's leather jacket.

Dom insisted that they stop in at a different store to what was Kiddo's routine, just in case some brazen daylight snatchers were hanging about his regular, less crowded haunts, and they wandered the aisles in search of Kiddo's desired ingredients for the night.

"*That's* how they spell shashlik for shashlik sticks?" Dom asked in surprise, taking the pack of wooden skewers from Kiddo and tossing it into the basket over his arm. "That doesn't sound like shazlick at all. I think I'll stick with 'kebab' to be safer."

"Do you think you'll ever have an opportunity to embarrass yourself by misspelling shashlik?" Kiddo raised his eyebrows at him.

"You just never know."

Kiddo selected the extra crunchy peanut butter jar for his satay sauce.

"Oh God yes," Dom moaned with orgasmic happiness. "Such a good choice."

"What if you're too excited by the food to focus over dinner talks?" Kiddo questioned with concern.

"I managed to hold it together over homemade dumplings even when I was half concussed," Dom answered reassuringly. "But the excitement level is real."

Dom then proved to be an efficient killer of cubed chicken, impaling the meat and dipping it all in the sauce while Kiddo chopped.

"Can I help with anything?" Sparks' voice came from behind them, and they turned to find her watching their progress as she leaned against the dining table.

Kiddo's stomach flipped and bounced. The choppy, jagged layers of her hair were defined with just the right amount of product. The tawny browns of her eyes stood out with a smoky liner that mesmerised him.

Dom greeted her with a warm, wide smile and sparkling blue eyes of his own that could have stopped a charging bull in its tracks. But he deferred to Kiddo – who was busy wondering how the two people he'd kissed last night weren't higher up on snatcher lists than he was.

"It'll be ready quicker if you're happy to get these onto the grill while I make more sauce," Kiddo quickly told her, a little breathlessly. "And Dom, you could steam the rice."

"More sauce?" Dom asked.

Kid shrugged at his typical forgetfulness. "Over compensating for forgetting to prep and marinade all this last night."

"The fact that you're making this now and finished your paper yesterday is triumph enough," Sparks chided him, knowing what he was thinking.

And he was so content between the two of them as he made the sauce and then threw together an omelette to add to Dom's rice, that he hardly registered the voices of the others as they gathered at the dining table.

He regarded the gang with surprise when he turned to find that the table was already set, with a jug of water and other assorted drinks put at different people's places, along with glasses out and serviettes folded.

"I did the cutlery," Quicklips told Kiddo proudly, and Velvet rolled her eyes and elbowed him.

But then she quickly jerked a sharp fingernail toward herself and mouthed: "napkins".

He plated up quickly, and Kiddo was more focused on the satisfaction on everyone's faces as they began eating at first, than he was on what Hato and Start were saying.

He blinked when Dom put a steadying hand on his bouncing leg, and forced himself to phase back into the conversation.

"They're definitely already arriving in droves," Jingle was telling them now. "Both the major and minor airports have had a high number of priority first class passengers or private plane arrivals. And a number of what will be rather out of place luxury mega yachts are scheduled to show up at the docks over the next few days. I'm collecting a list of potential reigning snatcher and high-rolling buyer names."

"I've been thinking over my stun grenade designs too," Trix chimed in then. "Sparks has helped me to make some prototypes, which worked pretty nicely on the snatchers I threw them at during patrol last night." She rubbed the back of her undercut then. "Though they kind of caused such paralysis that the snatchers just out-right died."

Seethe smirked. "But I bet they *were* stunned."

"I don't see a problem with leaving the prototype as is then," Tiny added gruffly. "We could just roll them down the ramp and see how many people we can shock to death." He shrugged.

"But there will be the snatched kids on show too," Trix reminded him. "I don't need that on my conscience."

"Nowadays snatched kids are tagged with a microchip immediately," Jingle mused. "I wonder if we can program the grenades so that their pulse incapacitates only people without that chip."

"That would knock out the ruling snatchers and the buyers, but all the minion snatchers would be protected along with the kids we're trying to help," Sparks mused.

"Alright," Jingle nodded. "We could try to make the programming specific. Newbie snatched kids would have a more general chip, like a sales tag or brand name. While fully fledged and initiated snatchers would have obvious identifiers, like a name or number. We could equip the grenades with smart scanners, but that'll mean we won't be able to make a whole heap of them, and we'll have to be very certain of the success rate of where we're putting them."

"If we're getting as complicated as all that, we need a general chip and a snatcher chip to work with," Trix stated firmly. "Too much is riding on getting these things right."

"The snatcher ID chip will be achievable," Flip set down his final empty skewer and scooped up a mouthful of rice. "But the general sales chip from a snatched kid will be near impossible."

"We do what we can do tonight, then," Seethe rocked his chair back and he squinted at them all. "We get a snatcher. We get a chip."

"Well don't just go and carve up the entire snatcher," Jingle told him flatly. "The chip will be the size of a grain of rice, and should be in the soft webbing of skin between the snatcher's thumb and forefinger."

Seethe shrugged. "We'll see."

"You can do clean-up duty then," Quicklips warned him huffily.

"That leaves the problem of how to get a snatched person's chip," Hato cut in with his low, steady voice.

There was the sound of Velvet tapping her nails against the tabletop, thinking.

"I think I have an idea about that," Sparks announced grimly. She pushed her plate away. "I've had more attempted snatchings here from The Lair than any of you so far. But this time we'll pretend to let it stick."

Kiddo's mouth dropped.

Everyone else but Dom was nodding and considering it.

"You or Velvet could make for good aesthetics bait," Flip agreed slowly. "Young. Easily both nines."

"Honestly, Velvet is the better fighter," Sparks said. "I'd prefer to know I have her out there making sure it really is just pretend."

Dom cleared his throat. "Actually, I was thinking I could offer up Raze," he suggested. "Raze would be valuable enough, and is a very wanted person. And while they know Hato and Seethe, they don't know me, so I can slip away after our little trap and stay as covert as ever."

Now Kiddo's jaw was hanging *and* his brow was furrowed.

"Nope," Kiddo heard himself speak as he was shaking his head, and all eyes turned to him. He almost never voiced anything while they were planning.

"Why does it have to be you two?" Kiddo went on, reddening. "They're after *me* already."

"Oh-ho," Flip tapped his chin. "The three of you together would be like bees to honey. The Lair will be the perfect place to contain it. Let them trickle in, spot the hottest threesome on the dancefloor. With a few great options as targets it's almost guaranteed they'll try to take and tag at least one of you through the night."

"And we'll cover every door and watch from every angle," Quicklips swore.

"Does it have to be The Lair?" Kiddo asked faintly. "The lights set me off."

Sparks reached to pat his hand. "Tonight is crooner's

night," she reassured him. "Soft mood lights and dramatic noir colours only."

"What?" Kiddo said in surprise. "Since when?"

"A year ago," Jingle gave a glowing smile and flicked her hair. "You wrote it on the program when you were putting it together as something different."

"You actually ran it? And are still running it?" Kiddo asked in surprise.

"Quarterly," Seethe affirmed dryly. Unenthused.

"It gives people a nice excuse to dress up in slinky evening-wear, and to slow down. Be romantic. It still gets pretty sexy." Surprisingly, it was Tiny who spoke then, rather dreamily. "And it gives Jingle a chance to perform. She's a great lounge singer."

"Hato kept running it in case you ever wanted to come down without fear of an episode," Sparks told Kiddo gently. "You'd proven your sobriety. It was only your fear of a fit holding you back."

"Anyone have anything other than black denim that I can borrow?" Dom asked thoughtfully then.

"I'm about your size," Flip nodded. "Both you and Kiddo can borrow some formal wear."

"And I've got the perfect dress for you, Sparks," Trix added, her eyes already crinkling as she envisioned it.

"I don't like this plan," Hato announced then. Crossing his arms. "Kiddo is too young. And it's a school night."

Everyone shared looks. And Kiddo felt a ball of resolve growing in his stomach.

"I'm only the youngest by a year," Kiddo replied calmly.

"I've patrolled plenty of times before, and I'm capable. I'm not really the kid who needs protecting."

Hato opened and closed his mouth.

His face became anguished.

"But," Hato began, his face earnest. "That was different. You weren't the one person they were specifically targeting. They weren't so desperate to collect."

"I can pull my weight as much as anyone," Kiddo told him almost gently.

"Hell yeah, you can," Quicklips affirmed – his eyes on his empty dinner plate as he absently rubbed at a spot on his muscle top. Definitely not peanut butter sauce. Definitely someone's makeup.

Kiddo tried not to get distracted by that. He would have to remember it later. And dab it with stain remover.

"I'll try to make sure it's me who gets nabbed," Dom told Hato. "Not one of yours."

"I don't like that either," Hato's great shoulders sagged. "You are one of ours now."

He eyed the rest of the gang balefully. "No snatcher under The Lair's roof slips through the cracks tonight. Nothing can go wrong."

| 21 |

Twenty One

"Mind if I do?" Dom asked Kiddo. They were leaning against the bar, taking everything in for a moment while they waited for Sparks.

Kiddo tore his eyes from the mood-lit, sensuous retreat that the craziness of The Lair had somehow become for crooner's night. All with just some well-placed, warm lighting on the stage that Jingle was absolutely owning. The black velvet drapes along the walls made everything else in the centre of the room seem bordered by a dream.

Nearly more dreamlike than the scene beyond their place in the hazy shadows, Dom was fitting almost too well into the suit pants and dress shirt that Flip had loaned him. He cut a sharp figure – dapper rather than tough without his leather.

"Stop eating me up with your eyes," Dom smirked, and then jutted his chin toward a drink that had been set in front of him.

"No, I don't mind at all," Kiddo remembered the original question. "Take the edge off."

"Have you partaken again at all since giving it up?" Dom

asked curiously, before tipping back his tumbler with a tinkle of shifting ice.

Kiddo shook his head. "Not a drop. But it won't do me any damage to smell it on you."

"Or taste it on me," Dom answered wickedly.

Kiddo felt his heart stutter. "That won't do me any harm at all."

Kiddo seated himself on a stool, immediately starting to rotate it from side to side with nervous energy.

Jingle's voice rolled over the intimate feeling space of the dancefloor in low waves. And all kinds of people – many who would normally be in there sweating and pulsing together savagely, were moving in slow, upright waves of their own. As if making love.

Everybody had made some kind of effort to neaten up. Hair was slicked back, shirts were pressed, dresses shone under the light, and hot coloured lipsticks sparkled bright on sultry lips.

Everyone else's movements were soft and languid. Kiddo tried to stop swivelling, pulling himself around to face the bar.

But that just made him notice Hato, hulking off to the side like the bouncer from hell in the distance. He knew Quicklips was at the entrance, monitoring who streamed down into the cellar-like club from the street above. Flip was leaning casually in the hallway that led to the bathrooms.

"Try not to see them," Dom advised. He put a hand to the back of Kiddo's neck and squeezed the tense muscles there in a kind of massage. "You don't know them tonight. And if they're doing their jobs properly, they won't be watching you, but everything around you."

Kiddo nodded, trying to make his shoulders relax as he turned toward Dom to hold his focus on him. He absently reached to tug at Dom's shirt, where a gap between the buttons was gaping so that there was a glimpse of lagoon blue ink below. He found that his touch brushed Dom's skin, and he paused, letting his knuckles graze Dom's sternum through the gap in the shirt distractedly.

For a moment he really did forget everything but the sight of Dom licking his lower lip and closing his eyes. But then Kiddo caught sight of Hato's stiff posture and meaty hand covering a likely scowling mouth, as if he were just cupping his mouth and chin in thought.

Kiddo snorted, and Dom followed his gaze.

"He doesn't want me to date until I'm finished school," Kiddo explained.

"Learning never stops," Dom commented wryly. "And he's totally ruining my 'they should be watching everything but us' theory."

"Should we explain that neither of us are hoping to settle down any time soon?"

Dom threw back the rest of his liquor with a grin. "Somehow I think that would make it worse."

Kiddo felt the tingle of fingernails run over his back and he shivered. "Neither of you are after commitment?"

"Not sure I'm completely capable of it," Dom answered, greedily drinking in the vision that was Sparks.

A burgundy, satin dress clung to her like Kiddo had never seen her overalls do. From scooped neck to mid-thigh, the material seemed to drip down her body, hugging to her curves like cool water that made him hot all over. Her hair had a wet-look style that she'd run her hands through to push it all backward in defined tousles. And he felt like he was dying.

"You're yours, he's his, and I'm mine," Dom almost crooned himself, his voice like velvet and his gaze like a hungry wolf's. "The perfect trio."

"Stop eating her up with your eyes," Kiddo jibed.

"Half the club is doing it," Dom shrugged with a grin.

"And the other half were looking at the two of you," Sparks replied. "Now let's go get noticed properly."

She reached for both of their belts, and pulled them from the bar, leading the way to the brightest part of the dancefloor.

Kiddo wished they could stay together in the shadows, just talking. Maybe touching. They could try that goodnight kiss again.

He had no idea how to do this sex-on-the-spot dancing everyone else was doing.

He was so aware of the other gang members watching. Their indistinct shapes on the peripheral of his vision, spinning there.

But then Dom twirled Sparks to face Kiddo. And Dom stood so close behind her, wrapping an arm around her middle. They were melded together, swaying already as if they could hardly help it, and Kiddo knew he had to get in on that.

Kiddo stepped forward as Sparks automatically put her hands on his chest, and he found himself reaching to take hold of her hips.

As if they were all magnetised, fitting together like well melded pieces, he was drawn into their motions. Her hips rotated under his hands, and the silkiness and firmness of her body pressed against his, while her movements right against Dom's groin must have been like ecstasy.

He even felt Dom's touch join hers on his chest, but instead of resting lightly on Kid's breastbone like Sparks' was, his hand bunched in Kiddo's shirt to pull him somehow even closer.

Sparks hooked one arm back around Dom's neck, dancing against him slowly without taking her eyes off Kiddo's face. The fingers of her free hand ran down his chest and stomach to rest on Kiddo's belt buckle. Holding him in place so that she had both Dom's hips and Kiddo's hips rubbing against her in a way that would surely spark a fire for real if they weren't careful.

Dom reached for one of Kiddo's hands then.

With total trust, Kid let Dom guide his own finger tips across Sparks' lips, then down the centre of her collarbones, and lightly over the skin above the slinky scooped neck of the dress.

When Dom let him go, Kiddo went on tracing her skin, up along the arm that she was hooking back up around Dom.

He finished by leaning closer again to kiss the side of her neck, behind her ear, and then lightly nipped her ear too.

He kissed a trail to her lips, and claimed them with his own.

She used Dom's body as an anchor to push against Kiddo more firmly – her lips dancing over his before she deepened the kiss, slowing it. Her leg was between his so that she undulated against his excitement, and he couldn't even have cared that she must have known.

Her hands were on either side of his face now. And he could taste her strawberry lipstick as if she had just bitten into the juices of the fruit itself.

He lightly gripped the base of her neck to press her mouth to his own more firmly, before pulling away.

She was breathless, her eyes glittering, her chest heaving against his in an unforgettable way.

Kiddo cupped her face warmly, leaning his forehead against hers for a few still moments, before he tilted her head toward Dom.

Dom obligingly guided Sparks' body with practiced hands so that she turned between them.

Dom sank down into a passionate kiss that made Sparks lean back on Kiddo for support – her bare shoulder blades now against him so that he could rub her skin and gently bite the top of one shoulder.

Kiddo felt the vibration of her groaning into Dom's kiss.

He smiled, because at the same time, he could feel Dom's finger curled around one of Kid's belt loops, forcing Kiddo to stay connected even as Dom kissed their girl.

And when he glanced up, Dom's eyes were on him. Making electric currents run up and down his skin in shocks.

"You three are hotter than hell!" someone called over the sultry music then.

A young man. Possibly a year younger than Kiddo. With a scar running down over his lip, and a wide smile curving it.

A girl, also around their age, with a high ponytail and rhinestone choker, smiled widely beside the young man too.

"Drinks?" she asked generously.

Sparks gripped the forearms of both Dom and Kiddo before they refused. In a normal world, you never accepted a drink from two strangers.

But tonight they had to play victims, not survivors.

"That is such a nice offer," Sparks gushed, "let's grab a lounge."

The girl made a show of delight that did not touch her face, reaching a hand out to grab Sparks' as if they were best friends.

Sparks made sure not to hesitate, reaching to take the girl's hand.

"Ouch," Sparks exclaimed.

"Oh, so sorry," the girl pouted, rubbing Sparks' hand in hers. "I *must* throw out this sharp ring."

Both Kiddo and Dom tried not to stiffen as Sparks slipped away from her cocoon between them – the girl pulling Sparks to a lounge with a circular silver table. A tray of exactly five drinks already waited conveniently for them.

"Hey, I'm Cayd," Kiddo managed to hold his own hand out to the guy with the scarred lip without baring or gritting his teeth.

"Great to meet you mate," the guy shook Kiddo's hand immediately, but Kiddo felt nothing.

"Ray," Dom lied, shaking hands too. "Like ray of sunshine."

"Nice! Let's join the girls!" This guy was way too chipper.

Dom shrugged his shoulders slightly in consternation. He hadn't felt anything either.

When they reached the table, Sparks was pretending to sip a fruity concoction of some kind, and they each did the same.

"Where are you all from?" the young man, who had not even bothered to give a false name to introduce himself, asked. "I've never seen the three of you together on that dance floor. I would remember it."

"We're …" Sparks rubbed her hand, and then her temples. She gazed at Kiddo and Dom for help.

"We're new. We don't really know anybody here," Dom provided. "It's so good to meet people and feel a bit safer and more connected in this city."

"So hard to be alone in this world," the girl was still smiling, running her fingers along her rhinestone choker.

"And you two? What's your story?" Dom asked.

Kiddo wrapped an arm around Sparks, who had begun to lean against him.

"Oh, we've been together for years. We're old news," the girl answered. "Nothing interesting."

The body language, angles and proximity suggested that these two individuals hardly knew, let alone cared for each other.

"Young love," Dom remarked. "I can feel it between you."

"But we're more interested in the three of *you*," the girl simpered. She reached toward Sparks, but her eyes lingered on Kiddo – sizing him up for every dollar he might be worth. "You're all so beautiful."

"Thank you," Dom took that one stoically.

Kiddo took Sparks' chin between his forefinger and

thumb. She had closed her eyes. But she had not touched her drink, and neither had Dom or Kiddo.

"Honey," the girl spoke to Sparks then with great care. "You don't look so well. Would you like me to take you to the rest rooms to freshen up?"

Even in a state where she was obviously being affected by something, Sparks stayed on the job. She nodded her head cutely, like a weak little lamb.

"Girls have to stick together," Sparks murmured sweetly.

And Dom and Kiddo were forced to let her go.

The other girl had to support Sparks' weight, as if she was too drunk to walk.

"A few drinks and they're wasted, hey," the guy tried for some conversation then. Ignoring the fact that Sparks' glass appeared full.

Kiddo tore his eyes from Sparks' retreating form when he saw Flip and Start, their two closest gang members, subtly watching everything like hawks.

"What do you do for a day job, *mate*?" Dom decided on a line of conversation of his own.

The guy took a big swig from his fruity drink. It *wasn't* laced.

"I work with other youth," the guy said at last. He eyed Kiddo. "Set them on their path."

Dom couldn't keep his mouth from pressing into a hard line.

The way the guy and girl had both been staring at Kiddo could have been flattering, if he hadn't known the real reason behind it all.

The song changed, and Kiddo thought he could hear a tiny hint of tension in Jingle's delivery now. Though she carried on like a star.

The guy's phone went off, and when he answered, he feigned a very surprised, concerned expression.

"Sure babe," he said, the word sounding unnatural. "We'll meet you out there."

He hung up.

"Everything alright?" Kiddo played along, trying not to sound too gruff.

"Turns out your friend isn't well at all. They've gone to get fresh air and need us to meet them outside."

Dom stood up abruptly, ready for the show to be over. "Well, let's do that then."

The guy quickly stood to lead the way. "They're just down the side street," he explained. "My girl has ordered us all a ride."

"Lovely." Dom was sickly sweet. "We appreciate it so much."

Kiddo noticed that Hato, Velvet, Quicklips and Frazzle had already disappeared. The others were hanging back, waiting to follow behind Dom and Kiddo.

The gang knew which way this was all going.

"Just out here," the guy promised, as they stepped up through the cellar doors, which were like storm doors, and out into the chill of the night. "Just down this alley."

| 22 |

Twenty Two

Kiddo was trying not to shake his head as he shivered. Why would anyone ever willingly follow a stranger who says "just down this alley"?

But then he saw Sparks on the pavement. She'd been leaned up against a brick wall, eyes closed and lips purple.

That was why.

That was why they hadn't needed to spike the drinks or do anything else. Choosing one friend to lure the others out worked well. And if they were just hunting an individual, pretending to help that person to get air would work too.

Kiddo hurried to Sparks, kneeling and taking her wrist in his hand to feel for a pulse.

"She'll be fiiine," the girl promised, coming to stand close to him. "Just sleeping it off." Her eyes flickered triumphantly to the road, and she seized Kiddo's arm, holding him as if he were her meal ticket.

There was a screech of tyres. A van was racing down the lane toward them. The driver probably thought the usual scream of patrol bikes would soon be hot on its tail-bar.

"Speedy pick-up car," Dom glowered, bunching his fists.

But as the van screeched to a halt at the kerb in front of them, there were flickers of motion on either side of the alley, closing off both sides.

Kiddo registered Start and Frazzle rolling out strips of nails to prevent a getaway.

The snatchers that Kiddo was used to seeing – masked creatures, were starting to climb limberly from the van. Two got out, before Trix sprinted at them with a ferocious cry, hurtling a grenade past them and into the open vehicle.

The two snatchers were surprised, but Trix tore their grips from where they still held the back doors open.

She pushed them backward and slammed the doors shut in their faces. There was an odd noise inside the vehicle, like the sound of a laser beam from a movie, and the van rocked as if in a strong gust of wind.

The masked driver, front passenger, and all movement from anyone else who had been in the van about to spring out, suddenly stilled. The driver and front passenger lolled in their seats, and there were a few thumping sounds as if people were slumping down dead in the back.

Flip and Seethe were tackling a couple of plain clothed snatchers who had also apparently exited the club to help with the snatch. The scar-lipped guy was lying with his eyes open at Dom's feet. And the female snatcher's hands were torn from Kiddo's arm. Her scream was cut short by Velvet's neat, lethal and extremely fast punch to compound the strongest of foreheads. It was all over in a jangle of Velvet's bracelets and bangles.

"You *bitch*," Velvet was saying. "What about girl code?"

Sparks had said that girls should stick together, but this one had apparently not cared.

"Velvet." Hato stopped Velvet from a second skull crushing punch. "You don't need to make a mess."

Hato and Frazzle had joined Kiddo by Sparks' side.

"Back to the club," Hato told Start, Quicklips and Velvet. "Tiny and Jingle are holding down the fort alone, and we don't know if other sharks were in there hunting."

They nodded, disappearing fast.

"You lot," Hato nodded at Trix, Flip and Seethe, who were blood spattered. "Clean up duty."

They nodded a little more grimly.

"Trix," Hato added. "Salvage their chips. And anything in that van you can find."

"Should we keep the van?" Flip asked.

But Hato shook his head. "They'll know which van belonged to the team that didn't come back. Using that van would be like screaming 'suspicious' in their faces."

Frazzle had checked Sparks' pulse too, and her eyes. "We move inside. Move is safe. Is drowsy drug. No long-term damage, remember?"

Dom stepped forward and tugged Hato's jacket. Hato quickly shrugged out of it so that Dom could have it, and Dom stooped over Sparks.

Kiddo helped to lean her forward so that Dom could thread her frozen arms through the giant sleeves, and when Kiddo lifted Sparks into a standing position, the jacket was longer on her than the slinky burgundy dress was.

"I've got her," Hato said grimly. His shirt looked fit to burst with protest as he flexed to pick her up, but he carried her effortlessly, as if she were his own child.

They carried her to her room, though she couldn't yet rouse to thank her lucky stars this time.

Instead, Hato left her tenderly wrapped up in his oversized jacket, let Kiddo undo the criss-cross straps of her heels, and tucked her in while Frazzle fetched his most delicate scalpel and tweezers.

Kiddo held Sparks' hand, where there was already a tiny nick in the skin between her thumb and forefinger, as Frazzle set about searching for the microchip.

"They must have pricked her with a dose of something along with the implant," Dom grimaced. "The drinks were clear."

"That's got to be a recent development," Kiddo frowned, thinking over the messy, physical nature of his own attempted abduction. "Or maybe only some of them are doing that."

"They adapt when they're desperate, I guess," Dom answered darkly. "They finally prefer not to have victims who struggle."

"You two still would have wound up marred by bruises if they planned to leave you aware," Hato growled. "They definitely didn't chip either of you?"

Dom double checked his own hand, shaking his head. "They were counting on us following them out to Sparks."

"Then they would've tagged and drugged you both when backup got out of the van," Trix announced from the doorway. Her hands were bloody, because she obviously hadn't taken as much care as Frazzle was taking of Sparks when re-moving chips.

"They were all be-jewelled with injector rings, pre-loaded with chips. No point them dealing with two heavy, passed out males before the cavalry arrived," Trix went on.

"Average weight, rather than heavy, thank you," Dom preened. "It's muscle mass."

"Good news is we have enough general victim chips for ourselves now," Trix ignored him. "If Jingle uses these as models and works out how to calibrate the grenades right, we should each be able to slip a chip into our pocket and avoid dying in any blasts."

"Still using 'ifs' and 'shoulds'," Dom stated unhappily.

"Give Jingle a little time," Hato reassured him. "She's more than just a sweet voice."

Frazzle set the grain sized microchip that he'd retrieved from Sparks' hand on his tray. "Need to work miracles," Frazzle commented with worry as he put a bandage over her skin. "Is so small chip to work with. How computer going to do anything with that?"

"Jingle can do it," Trix affirmed confidently, then stretched from where she'd been leaning in the door frame. "Just like you all did a great job being too hot to resist on that dancefloor."

"Very. So hot," Frazzle agreed with a blush. "Hard not to see."

Kiddo's face heated up in return.

"I'll sure be storing it in the memory banks," Trix tapped her head. "Anyway, perfect time for a cold shower." She held her bloody hands up with a shrug, then backed out to cross the hall for the bathrooms.

"Time we all left Sparks to rest," Hato announced firmly. "And went to our own beds."

Frazzle trailed after him to the door, and Kiddo reluctantly followed when Dom went without protest.

Hato switched off the light and closed Sparks' door with a click of finality, eyeing Kiddo and Dom sternly as they each went to their respective rooms.

But Kiddo had hardly glanced at his room, remembering the still broken shelf and pile of books from the following week, before Dom was tapping at his door.

"Ready?"

Kiddo blinked at him. "Ready for what?"

"We're going to tuck Sparks in properly so she knows she's safe."

"Hato –"

"Is such a dad," Dom smiled. "Come on."

Kiddo followed him without argument and quietly closed Sparks' door behind them as Dom crossed the room to her dresser.

"What are you doing? That's probably private," Kiddo scolded as Dom rifled through some things in the dresser, but selected a little pack of what Kiddo thought were tissues.

"Makeup wipes," Dom told him, drawing a few from the pack. "She doesn't want to sleep with her war paint still on."

Dom sat himself on Sparks' bed as if it were the most natural thing in the world. He rested her arm, with its barely visible hand still hidden in Hato's jacket, on his folded leg so that he could scoot closer. He tucked Sparks' hair behind her ear.

"Can you get a little light happening in here?" Dom asked.

Kiddo sighed, switching on the bed side lamp.

"Oh no," Dom shook his head. "Too bright. What if she wakes with a headache?"

"Too bright?" Kiddo echoed, his eyes searching for anything that could help. He settled on a blue, silk scarf that he had absolutely never seen her wear and that he had never washed for her. But it was draped over the mirror of her dresser all the same, and he drew the soft, floaty material down to settle it over her lamp shade.

"Mmmm, ocean scene," Dom approved as the room became a muted blue.

"More like lagoon scene," Kiddo corrected as he sat on Sparks' other side and took her other, bandaged hand. "Perfect for lotus flowers."

"And raging dragons," Dom agreed. He was very gently, patiently running a white little towelette over Sparks' skin, stroking across her brow, down the middle of her eyebrows and along her nose, delicately wiping her cheeks, her lips.

As his finger roved across her lower lip, she sighed and blinked awake.

"Hey gorgeous," Dom greeted her. "You're safe," he said, before panic could touch her eyes.

She took in what he had been doing, and that one of her hands was in Kiddo's, the other over Dom's knee. Her fingers tightened on them both. "Thank my lucky stars," she told them gravely.

"Thank mine too," Dom nodded, selecting a new wipe so that he could leave a cool trail down her neck and as far along her collarbones as Hato's wrapped jacket would allow.

"I was having fun until they interrupted," she commented. "That was the best dance of my life."

"That was the best dance in history," Kiddo uttered with a shiver. He realised he was still icy cold from the shock of the night, and the chill of the alley. His teeth chattered a little.

Dom's eyes flicked to Kiddo and he put his wipes aside. He rose, moving around the bed to stand at Kiddo's back, offering his own body warmth as he wrapped an arm around Kiddo from behind.

"You're still frozen," Dom commented, tracing his touch over Kiddo's shirt, and also over the hard nipples under that thin fabric, so that Kiddo froze in a different way.

Dom leaned further forward over Kiddo, and began to unbutton his way down Kiddo's front, his touch brushing Kiddo's skin and leaving trails of goosebumps.

"I'm not sure that will heat him up," Sparks mused, watching as Kiddo's chest and then taut stomach were exposed. Then she reached forward to take hold of Kid's belt buckle, undoing it, despite what she'd said.

However, Kiddo was suddenly feeling like he was burning alive.

"He's getting into bed," Dom explained. "And he's not going to ruin Flip's best clothes."

"This bed?" Kiddo asked, his heart thundering as he watched Sparks draw the zipper of his pants down.

"This bed," Dom affirmed. "And you're going to do your best to get a few hours of sleep in. Seeing as it's a school night."

Kiddo groaned, but Dom's hand came from behind to clamp over his mouth.

"Shush," he instructed. "We're not giving Hato any excuse to condemn us or to stop you from helping the gang when you want to."

Kiddo sagged back against Dom, and nodded into his hand before Dom let go.

Then Dom took a hold of Kiddo's shirt and stripped it backward so that Kiddo felt the air rush around him and he shivered again.

When Dom withdrew to lay the shirt out across Sparks' dresser, Kiddo resignedly rose to remove his shoes, socks and pants, setting them neatly aside too.

Dom was disrobing now as well, and as he stepped out of his trousers, Kiddo realised that it was the first time he had caught an almost unobstructed view of the artistry that was Dom's physique.

"Beautiful," Sparks voiced Kiddo's opinion appreciatively. She was propped up on her elbows against the pillows.

From the first scar and tendril of ink behind his ear, to the weaving, borderless patterns of playful fish, lotuses on flowing water, and bold dragons shooting plumes of flame over his back, around his pectorals, and down his ribs to disappear beneath his underwear line – the lagoon scene continued to wrap about him without changing in theme.

But Kiddo could now see that what must have been a terrible burn raked its way from hip level down to back of the knee level on his left side. It snaked around the front in a few places too, and there were more silvery marks dashed across his calf. At that point, the lagoon scene changed to encompass the marks in a new way.

The new scene not only incorporated the scars, but glorified them. Celebrated their ferocity. They became part of a twisting, surly storm of otherwise only black and white inks. They were part of the dark, or sometimes silvery edges of roiling clouds and forked lightning. The scene was ominous and brave all at the same time. And as Sparks had said – beautiful.

Dom stepped toward Kiddo to push him toward the bed. But Kiddo couldn't help reaching out to trace the goose-bumped, patterned flesh standing out on Dom either.

Dom stilled as Kiddo's fingertips followed a koi tail over his ribs and under his arm, and then traced the tail of the dragon with the burning eyes, his touch looping around Dom's own nipple as it stiffened.

Then Kiddo gripped Dom's shoulder and dragged him forward for a ragged kiss that tore at Dom's lips and pushed at his tongue.

When Kiddo had finished, Dom leaned breathlessly against him for a moment, arm now thrown over Kiddo's shoulder in a half embrace.

"That stopped you," Kiddo observed, drawing Dom toward the bed. "Not one jolt or mindless fidget for a few seconds," he teased.

Dom grinned as he recognised his own words. "A good-night kiss always works."

Sparks drew the blanket aside for Dom to slip in beside her, and she 'oohed' at how chilled Dom's skin was as he settled on his side to spoon her.

Kiddo circled the bed and slid in on her other side. He felt Dom's arm, where it had snaked inside Hato's jacket so that his hand could rest on Sparks' satiny stomach.

Dom lifted his arm a little, so that Kiddo could ease his own hand in to hold Sparks' hip, with Dom's arm crossing over his in a warm connection too.

"Dom?" Sparks said.

"Mmm?"

"You are one of the best things to have happened to us," she told him softly.

"That's a nice thing to say," Dom answered just as softly.

"It's true," Kiddo agreed, and he felt Dom's arm shift so that instead of crossing wrists, Dom was now resting a hand over Kiddo's on Sparks.

"Maybe you're mine, she's mine and I'm mine?" Dom murmured.

"Maybe you're ours."

| 23 |

Twenty Three

He woke to Dom, who was still mussed with sleep himself, shaking his shoulder.

"This is not going to be a good day for you and your issues with focusing," Dom told him quietly, holding up Kiddo's school clothes and satchel. "That was not enough sleep."

Kiddo went to sit up in a bleary panic, but Dom held him down and nodded his head at Sparks – still resting.

"We need to rush in a fluster, but we need to do it *quietly*," Dom instructed, and Kiddo nodded, edging out of the bed.

"You grabbed these from my room?" Kiddo whispered, pulling on his uniform. "Thank you."

Dom looped Kiddo's tie around his neck for him and tightened it – enough to be neat, but not constricting. "Got to help you get through school if you can't date 'til you're finished," he grinned evilly.

Kiddo forgot to feed Duncan Jr., he didn't grab his shopping list, and he only remembered his shoes because Dom pointed his socked feet out to him. But he was only two minutes late as he flew into class, and surely –

"Two minutes is still late," the teacher told him. "I've already marked the roll."

And the day was not off to a good start.

"You've written one word in all that time?" his teacher asked him next – disbelief on the man's face.

Kiddo hadn't even been talking to anyone, which was what it took for normal kids to waste time, and the instructions had been incredibly clear. But, apart from the one lone word on Kiddo's page, the other words that should now be with it had been playing chasey in his head, and climbing over the wrinkles of his brain like it was a jungle gym.

"Sorry sir," Kiddo muttered, watching everyone else leave. "I'll make it up."

"Was there something else on your mind?"

Kiddo stared at his desk, his leg bouncing.

How could he say that he'd been thinking about how much he thought he loved Hato? Frazzle. Flip. All of them. Including Seethe and Velvet.

Especially Sparks.

And how he was certain he loved Dom.

How could he say that he was worried they might all die this weekend?

Dom had said they were all Raze. All standing up to wage war on the snatchers. But they were so few, against so many.

"No, thanks for asking sir," Kiddo answered. "I'll make up for the work."

The teacher nodded, regarding him seriously, and Kiddo scooted out from the desk to hurry from the room to his next class down the hall.

"You're late."

"Sorry, I was with Mister –"

"You can make it up after school."

Kiddo grimaced.

Hato had chosen a strict, regimented school for a reason. But it sure hurt.

"Debasing your textbook covers is hardly stellar academic work. Is that all you managed to do in all that time?" this teacher asked him at the end of class too.

Kiddo glanced at his cover. A grenade, a grain of rice and the question 'how to get in??' were scrawled on the page.

He was confident that Jingle, Trix and Sparks would be able to produce their grenade weaponry and their little pieces of microchip armour. Yet it all meant nothing if they had no way of using those things.

"Where are today's equations?" the teacher prompted.

Kiddo swallowed. The numbers had been evading him – doing laps and cannonballs as if his mind was a swimming pool on the hottest day in summer.

But one thought had been sticking with him.

A sick thought.

About how Kiddo himself might be the ticket to getting into the snatcher stronghold.

"Sorry," Kiddo mumbled, grabbing his things. "See you after school."

It was a short detention, but now that he'd dealt with the thoughts that had been jostling to be at the forefront of his mind, they had receded, and he was able to fly through the work he should have been doing in his classes, stringing the words and numbers together as needed.

He slung his satchel over his shoulder, his mind half somewhere else as Dom dropped down from the gate pillar to land beside him.

"Rough day?" Dom asked, grabbing Kiddo's satchel and carrying it for him. "I thought we would leg it today."

"Sure." Kiddo surprised Dom by quickly looping an arm around his neck and pulling him into a hug before releasing him. "This will be the best bit of the day."

Dom was grinning as they set off down the street, but he frowned when they got closer to the warehouse.

"Hey," Dom said then. "Don't you normally pick up fresh ingredients for dinner when you get out of school?"

Kiddo raised his eyebrows. "Oops." He shrugged. "My brain is elsewhere."

Dom regarded him closely. "Are … you good?"

"I'm fine," Kiddo promised. "I'm good."

The others stared at Kiddo in shock when Dom explained that pizzas were getting delivered instead of their usual homemade variety.

"You forgot to get dinner?" Seethe asked, wearing a frown similar to the one Kiddo's teachers had been aiming at him all day.

"*We* forgot," Dom corrected. "But we're getting takeout."

"But the food," Quicklips said worriedly to Kiddo. "It's your thing, man."

Rather than setting the table, Kiddo was already seated beside Sparks, while Dom pointedly handed plates to Start and Velvet.

Frazzle fed Duncan Jr. when it became apparent that nobody else was.

"Have you been taking your meds?" Hato questioned.

"Yes," Kiddo waved him off. "I'm *fine*. I've just been thinking."

Everyone but Dom exchanged glances.

"Pizza's here," Dom announced brightly, spotting them from the window. He tugged on Tiny's arm so that Tiny begrudgingly followed him down to the garage level to help.

Everyone was seated uneasily when Dom and Tiny re-entered and set the boxes down.

"Pizza being here normally creates more excitement," Dom remarked, taking his seat on Kiddo's other side.

He opened a box and snavelled a piece, glancing around at the others in consternation.

Kiddo followed suit. Not meeting anyone's eyes.

He chewed for a moment. Swallowing much too loudly in the silence.

"So ..." Kiddo managed to begin then. "I think I'm our best chance of getting someone else down into the snatcher expo," he announced. "We have to let me get snatched, and have someone else blend with the snatchers who do it."

A blob of cheese dribbled off the tip of Dom's pizza, where he held it poised and ready for a bite.

"You're joking," Hato glowered. "You played your part last night."

"If we let it happen Thursday night," Kiddo went on, "they won't have long to mess me up, but just long enough to process me for entering into the competition. And I'll only miss one day of school."

Hato pushed his plate away from himself brusquely. "There'll be another way."

Velvet flashed Hato a hard look. "You said when you got home just before that you were out of ideas. Now you have one."

"A bad one," Flip negated.

Start scratched his head guiltily. "We're all going to need to wind up getting down there and into harm's way eventually. We need something that'll cause a stir, like Kiddo's arrival, to help us get one hidden person in the door first. The rest can follow."

"But Kiddo would be in there, not hidden or safe at all, alone, with snatchers, for *two* nights before the expo even starts." It was Jingle who was shaking her head now.

Kiddo gave her an imploring look. "I have every faith that you, Trix and Sparks will be able to come up with something that will have enough of an impact to change the direction of the snatcher industry forever. But being snatched is what *I* can do to help."

Her shoulders slumped, and she sat back silently, pushing her pizza around her plate.

"Kiddo was their main goal last night," Tiny rumbled. "They couldn't take their eyes off him."

"Nobody could take their eyes off any of them," Velvet added. "It was one of the hottest things I've ever seen in that club."

"But especially him," Tiny shrugged. "Like they'd found the holy grail."

"Kiddo's arrival just might cause enough excitement, that

someone very good at sneaking in could go under the radar as a fake snatcher," Seethe turned his empty beer bottle in his hands. "Then that person could smuggle information out to us. Help us work out how it's all going to look, where to hit and how to get in."

"I'm that person," Dom spoke up then. "The slipperiest spy you never saw until I wanted you to."

Kiddo smiled at Dom, though a little sickly. He rubbed his sweaty palms on his school trousers over and over. Sparks gripped his knee.

"Dom and I can do this," Kiddo said certainly, if unhappily. "I mean, Dom already has that mask."

"And we'll be getting you back," Quicklips promised. "That'll be another two nights this week without a home-cooked dinner."

"We'll all be coming back from this," Hato vowed. "Otherwise, what's the point to it all?"

He didn't mean the point to standing up to the snatchers.

He meant the point to everything and anything at all.

"When we find our kind of people," Dom agreed. "We do everything we can to keep them alive."

| **24** |

Twenty Four

The next day went by in a haze, much to the disappointment of Kiddo's educators. But with Dom's help he remembered to sort out dinner and got through that.

Now Kiddo was towel drying his hair, with a toothbrush in his mouth and another towel around his hips, when he spotted Dom in the mirror – leaning in the bathroom doorway.

"Let's get out of here for a bit," Dom suggested.

Kiddo gave an exaggerated look down at himself.

"Once you're appropriately decked out."

Kiddo rinsed. "But it's a school night," he admonished dryly, putting his toothbrush away.

"It's Wednesday night. Possibly the last school night of your young life if things go awry tomorrow night," Dom answered flatly. "Let's get out of here for a bit," he repeated cajolingly.

Kiddo crossed from the bathroom to his bedroom to dress, while Dom waited with his hands jammed in his leather jacket pockets, eyeing the shelf and books on the floor.

"I can fix that sometime," he said.

"I haven't been in here often enough lately to remember to do it," Kiddo admitted bashfully, sifting through his wardrobe for a jacket.

"Put on something with a hood," Dom said then. "And keep it drawn up."

Kiddo grabbed a hooded jacket as instructed, and pulled it on.

"Are you the restless one tonight?" Kiddo asked.

Dom moved to the window. "If this is how amped up you usually feel, I'm sorry. I feel like I can hardly contain myself."

"Sounds about right," Kiddo nodded sympathetically. "Jittery to the point of combustion on a normal day." He came to stand beside Dom, gazing out at the street. "But I think the others are feeling pretty similar right now too."

Dom sighed. "They've known you so much longer than I have, and of course they love you and are worried too."

Kiddo felt a warm rush of tingles all over at the 'too' bit.

"But I'm so worried for you that it *hurts*."

"I'm not the only one to be worried about in this whole venture," Kid said. "I'm worried I'm going to lose one of them. Or you."

Dom sighed again. "So let's get out, get ourselves ready, get rid of this energy."

He pointed a finger at a car parked across the street then. It had only recently been defrosted, with a glistening, fresh film over it, and steam curling up from its bonnet.

"I just parked that there," Dom told him. "It's unlocked, and not known in this area."

"That is *not* your car," Kiddo reproached. "We could have used one of Hato's from the garage."

"Hato's cars are known, and he's been quietly dodging attacks all week," Dom replied calmly. "I borrowed the car from little Miss Dorris at Ochre Way. She only drives it on Sundays to church, and won't even know it's been borrowed."

Kiddo gaped silently.

"I'll leave her some petrol money on the dash if you're worried," Dom put his hands up placatingly. "Though it'll only confuse her."

"Hato's been facing attacks?"

"Oh," Dom understood then. "Little skirmishes so far. I've helped him out a few times. They struggle to get at him though, because it's hard to predict which post he'll take at night, he's surrounded in you lot and a whole lot of patrons, or armed to the teeth on patrol. They would never do something blatant at The Lair, where so many youthful prey gather. So, they can only try and catch him out by day, where there are very few covert opportunities, and he rarely heads out anyway."

"Do the others know?" Kiddo frowned.

Dom put a hand on his hip. "I *told* you all that he's got a target on his back. I wasn't lying." Then he softened. "But he keeps a tight lip. Seethe happened to be with him the first time, and has taken up going with him almost everywhere since. I just fluked being nearby that time and a couple of others – and that's the main reason I know."

"Alright," Kiddo shook his head with eyebrows raised. "We don't take one of our cars then."

"Definitely not," Dom answered. "Miss Dorris has provided. Now as soon as you're down the fire escape, get straight in the back seat and lie down."

"Lie down?" Kiddo crossed his arms. "What if we get pulled over?"

Dom wedged the window up. "I'd rather talk to the cops about my sleepy friend in the back, than have the wrong person spot you as we're driving along, and get Miss Dorris' car rammed off the road."

"Ok," Kiddo gave in. "I'll lie down. Don't want to get snatched too early."

"Thank you," Dom answered sincerely. Then he paused, eyes on the street as he waited for something.

A moment passed, and then one of the gang cruised by watchfully on their bike, the motor purring.

"Now, after you," Dom said gallantly when the bike had roved by.

Kiddo nodded, and then moved fast – swinging himself over, and then using his hands on the rails to half slide and half step fast down the stairs.

He didn't wait when his sneakers touched down on gravel, but ghosted his way across to Miss Dorris' car, climbing straight in and sprawling out across the back.

Dom was in the front seat just a moment later, starting the car and getting them onto the road.

Dom's eyes flicked over Kiddo in the rear-view mirror, a startling blue as they were framed in light by a passing car's reflected headlights. He grinned.

"I'd prefer you spread out in the back of my car if I wasn't driving," he said cheekily.

"It's not your car," Kiddo reminded him.

"For Miss Dorris' sake, it's lucky I'm driving."

Dom took a number of turns past signs that Kiddo did recognise, but also took turns he didn't recognise from his angle, where he could only catch names of streets and factory buildings.

Dom's eyes went frequently to the rear-view mirror, but also often roved back over him, now laid out with his arms behind his head and his shoes impolitely up on the seat.

Kiddo was surprised when the car cruised to a stop inside what appeared to be an abandoned shed, based on its lopsided roof. He sat up and opened the door to step out into a fresh breeze of salty air.

The little car was tucked away and nicely hidden in a disused boat shed that had fallen into disrepair.

"That was a round-about way to get to the docks," Kiddo commented, surprised that that was where they'd ended up.

Dom came around and reached up to pull Kiddo's hood a little lower.

"Evasive driving, little old lady style," Dom informed him. "We're not far from where we're going."

Kiddo followed him out, keeping to the shadows as Dom headed to a high wire fence.

"I recognise this fence," Kiddo whispered over the sea wind.

They scaled it together quickly, their fingers stinging as they gripped the diamond shaped criss-crosses of wire, trying not to rattle the whole fence on the way back down.

"I recognise this tunnel," Kiddo whispered again, before he skidded down and then caught the back of Dom's jacket to keep him from shooting all the way out to the other side of the cement cylinder and into the sloshing water.

"I brought Hato here," Dom confessed.

"You did?" Kiddo squished up his face, as if this ugly pipe was sacred to the two of them alone.

"It wasn't a neat fit," Dom assured him. "But I brought him here so that he could see what I had seen, without realising it, on the night you stowed us here."

Dom gestured to the lapping water side of the tunnel, and the small waves were all that Kiddo noticed at first. But he peered beyond that when Dom kept watching his face expectantly.

Kiddo strained his eyes across the wide expanse of water. The other side of the round inlet, which in daylight was lined by busy piers that jutted along the whole of the docks, was in near darkness. Totally still and shapeless.

And then Kid felt his blood run cold when he saw the darkness momentarily interrupted by a glittering speck of light. It was there, then it was gone.

It was like a trick, and Kiddo wondered if he had really seen it. But there it was again, and then it was gone once more.

A few moments later, moving extremely slowly, headlights on surely illegally low beams rolled into view, pausing at the flickering light.

Kiddo started when the light flickered rapidly a few times, before the headlights rolled forward, seemed to angle downward, and then abruptly disappeared.

"You just saw a snatcher van scan for entry into the hidden ramp in the pipe pile," Dom confirmed grimly. "You're looking at the entry to where thousands of uncared for youths go missing each year. Where you will be taken tomorrow night, no matter how cared for you are."

"You were never uncared for," Kiddo shivered. "You were just lost."

"I will not lose you," Dom stated firmly. "I wanted you to see, just in case, that you know this area. If you need to get loose, and manage to do it, you know how to get away on the surface."

"Then their whole base stretches out below ground level?" Kiddo asked.

"As far as I can tell, it runs all the way from the water's edge to that warehouse called Cargo Bay over there," Dom answered. "It runs under Cargo Bay, which provides a storage space for them. And as we thought, they load onto ships that get close enough to the water side of those pipes."

"How deep do you think it all goes?" Kiddo frowned. "How big is the complex?"

Dom scowled. "Jingle pointed out that all of the snatchers you've ever dealt with and unmasked, have never had an identity above ground."

"They don't live on the surface," Kiddo realised with a shock. "They don't officially exist up here?"

"Once they're turned to snatchers, they cease to be anyone or anything but that," Dom affirmed. "There must be hundreds of them down there, living the underground life."

"They never seem close to each other, or to care about

each other," Kiddo remarked in surprise. "I can't believe they live in such a community."

The two snatchers from The Lair had been operating as a couple, but there had been absolutely no feeling there.

"Care is beaten out of them," Dom glowered. "They learn to do the job, and to survive for themselves."

Kiddo's brain couldn't grasp how far back from the docks the base must stretch, let alone how wide out it might reach on either side. They would be able to fit everything a society might need down there.

One side was protected by water, the other side was protected by layers of earth. The single entrance was so hidden, nobody had ever picked up on it before.

And this was just one base in one major city of the world. There would be others. All over the globe. There really wouldn't be a chance like this to deliver them a blow for another ten years.

Shit.

"Another indicator of how damn big it is down there," Dom went on, "is the fact that Jingle hasn't picked up on any increase in guests at nice hotels."

Kiddo gaped. "So all of the reigning snatchers and their followers, as well as their competition entries, are all able to fit down there too?"

"Seems so," Dom granted. "And I can bet the reigning snatchers would each only stay in the greatest of comfort with plenty of space."

"How in the world is Jingle going to pull off a grenade pulse big enough to take down an operation that size?" Kiddo slumped back against the rounded tunnel wall.

"She's been briefed. She's confident. Talking about things like scanners and waves. Let's leave that to her to figure out," Dom suggested.

Kiddo nodded. "Thanks for warning me of what I might expect." He swallowed. "Where I'll be going."

Dom angrily slouched down, fitting his back against the curved concrete tunnel wall, and thrusting his legs outright so that his boots were resting up against the tunnel roof.

Kiddo shuffled down too, resting his own shoes on the wall of the tunnel beneath Dom's.

"Can you tell me what to expect when they take me down there?" Kiddo asked carefully then. "Do you remember much?"

Dom drove his knuckles against his eyeballs as if he could also drive out the memories. "Do I ever ..." he puffed out a massive breath of air before lowering his hands.

Kiddo rested his shoulder so that it was touching Dom's, and waited for him to go on.

"There was the cable tying in the van," Dom began. "You might not get that, if they've moved on to sedatives. But they still might to be safe."

Kiddo took and patiently unfurled Dom's hand, which had gone white with the pressure of the fist he had been making.

"You'll be feeling hazy, and there are no windows in the van," Dom continued. "When they drag you out, you'll be given a cursory glance by a lead snatcher, but while it's rare to be seen by an actual reigning snatcher at this point, you might cause enough of a stir to warrant it."

Dom watched Kiddo, who was rubbing and warming one of Dom's hands between the two of his own.

"You'll be taken to a clinic room next, where a physician will examine you. You will not be given your clothes back, but will be given something that could count as underwear. Because of the aesthetic nature of the competition, I can imagine that every inch of you will be measured and critiqued. Beauty is in the eye of the beholder, but the judges will also have had to come up with actual criteria they can mark you against, which will guide the physician and reigning snatchers' examination. Don't fight them at this point, if you're lucid enough to do so. It's worse if you do. Instead, tell them you have epilepsy, and they might try to give you something to mask the symptoms, which will help you to avoid an episode."

Kiddo realised he was now repetitively rubbing his hand against Dom's, creating heated friction, and he tightly squeezed his fingers through Dom's to still himself.

"Then you'll be taken to the halls of holding cells, where stock usually wait for sale and then shipping. It's like a vault of capsules, each little capsule with three cushioned walls at the back and sides, and a padded low ceiling and floor to keep panicked snatched kids from doing themselves harm. The front wall looks out onto the hall so that the snatchers can always see what's going on in each cell – that wall is made of very thick glass, and is where the door and a slot for air or trays of food is fitted. Trust me, you can't use that glass or the door to help you get out. Don't bother trying. You'll only be able to get free by yourself if they open the door for some reason. Or when I come and get you."

Kiddo was still squeezing Dom's hand and he tried to relax.

"It's all very clean, to prevent you from getting sick before reaching your buyer. There's even a covered cube to sit on in the corner, and if you lift the top, it's actually a toilet. The worst thing about the clinical setting of the cells, apart from the fact that you're there against your will, is that they keep the lights on without fail – and everything is almost blindingly white so that you and any bit of grime are visible."

Dom was squeezing his hand right back. They were making one big, tight fist between the two of them now.

"I'm guessing they are going to be using those holding cells for all of the competition entries until it's show time. So you'll be surrounded in beauty. But they blindfold you and tie you any time they have to move you from your capsule. Because of that I never saw anything else about the process, so I can't guess at what you'll face for the expo."

Kiddo rubbed his spare fingers over both of their knuckles. He couldn't think of anything to say.

"Kiddo," Dom started, after a quiet pause.

"Yeah?"

"I promise, I'll do everything in my power to be unnoticed so I can stay close to you. And I will do everything in my power not to lose you." His hand lost some of the strength behind his tight hold on Kiddo's. "I will memorise every step of that place for the gang, and will always find my way back to you."

"No fear," Kiddo uttered.

"Oh, still a ton. But I feel better that you know what I'm promising."

Kiddo gave him a half smile. "You'll have me back for school on Monday, I'm sure."

"Or Hato will," Dom shrugged. "He's focused enough on your education for the three of us."

Dom watched Kiddo tapping a sneaker against the tunnel wall rhythmically. He was mulling something over, and Kiddo let him.

"Kiddo," Dom began again, delicately. "You said Hato doesn't want you dating yet. But you also said that you were … experienced."

Kid gave a nod. "I used to be a little skeleton, rutting around in the filth with anyone who could pay," he answered honestly. Glumly. "How messed up is that?"

"It makes me sad," Dom told him, his blue eyes intense on their hands. "Did you ever make love for real after that?"

Kiddo's sneaker stopped tapping. "I can't say I've ever made *love*."

Dom nodded. "Did you ever want to?" he asked curiously. "Are you still interested in that, after your introduction to it all?"

Kiddo considered it. He considered the number of times he could have made a move on Sparks, and how he'd wanted to. He thought of how often she had got close to making a move herself, but how she had never pushed.

He thought of Dom.

"Sparks used to be the only one who made me think that feelings like that might still be possible," Kiddo answered. "Now, with you, I'm learning they definitely are." He cocked an eyebrow. "Which means I'm also learning that I don't just like girls."

Dom turned on his side, leaning up on an elbow over Kiddo.

Kiddo gazed up at Dom's face. Bruised, solemn, gorgeous.

"I hope we live long enough for me to explore that with you," Dom stated. "*And* girls. We would make such a team."

"We already do."

When they finally crept back out of the tunnel and drove back to Mrs Dorris' place, with Dom leaving a twenty dollar note on her dash to confuse her, they took a mix of main streets and unknown streets to get back toward the warehouse lanes. Then they took to the rooves until they got closer to home.

After their sprint to safety, Dom was tired enough that he crawled straight onto Kiddo's bed to pass out on top of it. But Kiddo covered him with his own half of the blanket, knowing he was never going to be able to close his eyes himself.

Instead, he went to the library level.

Just like the night he had first seen the vision that was Dom, he left the room dark except for the silver glow of the night sky through the arched window.

He set out the journals he wanted to work on – all of the club orders, budgeting and general household paperwork. He wanted to give them one good hyper focus before he was taken. Just in case he wasn't coming back.

| 25 |

Twenty Five

Kiddo's eyes didn't even feel like sandpaper when he closed the journals as the sun came up.

He felt awake and oddly calm.

Set.

Kiddo went downstairs to feed Duncan Jr. and to start the coffee, which Velvet would be needing after patrol.

He ate a piece of toast while starting to butter a stack for Quicklips and anyone else who would be wandering down soon.

He grabbed his shopping list, and made sure to zip it into his satchel when he went back upstairs.

He brushed his teeth without hurriedly splattering toothpaste everywhere. He combed his hair. He remembered after-shave. He took his meds.

He crept into Sparks' room, and kissed her lips so lightly that she smiled in her sleep. She had already pressed her snooze button.

"I love you," he whispered beside her ear.

"Love you too, Kiddo," she sighed back.

His school shirt was fresh, un-crinkled and buttoned correctly, with his tie in place and everything else ready when he woke Dom.

Dom wasn't as gentle at waking slowly as Sparks, but he was getting better at not waking up with fists flying.

"Wow," Dom complimented him after he rubbed his eyes. "Nothing like a life-threatening event on the horizon to make a kid smarten up for school."

When they were nearing Kiddo's campus, Dom walked backwards, a little ahead of Kiddo so he could look at him.

Then Dom reached to flick Kiddo's collar up against the wind, using his grip on it to make Kiddo walk right into him, into a kiss.

"Have the best day you can," Dom told him. And then let Kiddo leave him for first class.

"I'm going to be absent tomorrow," Kiddo told his morning teacher, coming in ahead of the bell. "Can I collect the work now?"

"You're always late, but rarely absent," the teacher answered, but began writing a few dot points of what he would need to catch up on. "Is everything alright?"

"I'm fine sir," Kiddo told him. "Thanks for the list."

This time, when the words he needed were locked behind a heavy door – he broke it down and wrangled them into order.

"I'm going to be absent tomorrow," Kiddo told his next teacher. "Can I collect the work now?" He handed over the list of dot points to be added to for this subject.

"Absent as well as always tardy? How is it that you keep

winding up top of all your classes?" his teacher lamented, but wrote some tasks down anyway.

This time, when the numbers were behaving like a bunch of monkeys escaping from the zoo, he caught them and forced them into line.

The teacher nodded approvingly, glancing at Kiddo's page. "That's why you top your classes." Then moved on.

By the end of the day, Kiddo had compiled everything he would need to do on Sunday night if he was still alive and able to get ready for Monday.

Take summary notes for the chemistry test.

Write a plan for an essay question. Include quotes.

Answer the equations for exercise seven.

Revise the history of the United Nations and its policies on human rights. That was quite relevant.

Read pages eight to twelve of his 'Modern World Legal' text.

"That is a very heavy satchel," Dom assumed a winded expression as he tried to lift it against Kiddo's back.

"I'm remaining optimistic that I'll still need all those texts," Kiddo informed him.

"All those texts will weigh down the bike," Dom said. "I hope you don't need much from the store."

Dom tried to remain upbeat as they made chicken and fried rice together. Sparks helped them ladle it out. But the rest of the crew were struggling for any kind of positivity as it was served up to them.

"Have you worked it out yet?" Tiny asked Jingle gruffly.

"I'll work it out," Jingle sniped back in a 'back-off' kind of tone.

"Seethe has collected me a nice little snatcher wardrobe over the last couple of nights," Dom changed the topic.

"Reminds me," Seethe sucked his teeth as he pulled something from his back jeans pocket. He threw some leather fingerless gloves across the table to Dom. "They'll cover the lotus tattoo on your hand, in case they've heard the Raze rumours about Miss Lotus' artwork like Flip had."

"Thanks," Dom told him, rising to get a cloth to wipe some crusted blood from the right glove. "That completes the ensemble."

"Jingle put together one of my designs for a gadget you can use, like the old style spies used to have," Trix added then.

"Lipstick gun?" Dom asked, delighted. "Or shoe phone?"

"Actually, it's a laparoscopic camera that they use for surgeries," Jingle informed him, a little less harried after a few mouthfuls. "It's embedded into the belt buckle that you'll be wearing, and will automatically record and take snap shots. I've also put a general snatched-victim chip in there to keep you safe."

"*That* will complete the ensemble then," Dom nodded. "I doubt you had top surgical equipment just lying around though?"

"Don't ask," Trix grimaced. "It was an emergency. But that one is definitely on my conscience."

"If you manage to get reception, you'll be able to use a snatcher issue phone or computer to Bluetooth the files to yourself and then to us," Jingle went on. "I don't know if they only use their tech on the surface, or if they actually work so far down in their hovel. But you'll find out."

"Aim your crotch toward any key passageways and spaces so we can throw together a rough floor plan," Flip suggested. "The belt buckle will do the rest."

"I've also got something else you shouldn't ask about," Trix told Dom. She set a small green, pocket-sized pack on the tabletop and slid it across to him. "They're military grade."

It looked like a pack of the kind of mint strips that dissolved on your tongue.

"Thanks," Dom told her. "But I'm still eating."

"No, dummy," she snickered. "These tiny strips are highly reactive once air-born. They're still experimental, and haven't been released for military use yet. But I've made sure the pack has a good clip on the lid, which dispenses one at a time, so as long as that's shut, you're fine."

Dom pulled a face as he gingerly accepted the mint case.

"Basically, if you want to create a fiasco, stick one of these babies where you want it. It takes fifteen seconds or so for the air to melt the ingredients, and it'll only leave a little crater behind, but it will definitely distract with a bang," Trix informed him.

"Very handy. Now to remember not to go chowing down on mint wafers," Dom answered, making a mental note.

"Kiddo," Jingle called Kid's attention back to her as he rose from the table with his empty dish. "I *will* work my end of things out too."

He gave her a smile. "I know."

"We'll all be there," Tiny added then.

Kiddo glanced around at Hato, Frazzle, Quicklips – all of them.

Sparks' face was stony and tough, which he knew meant she was trying not to be emotional.

Velvet was glowering down at her dinner, pushing a piece of chicken around with her fork.

"I know you will."

| 26 |

Twenty Six

Kiddo took his time meandering to the bus stop shelter the next block over from the warehouse.

He knew Dom would already be hidden in the shadows somewhere there.

"Ahh shittt," he breathed to himself as he sat down like a vulnerable lamb under the shelter, feeling like the streetlight overhead was a spotlight. Nobody could miss him.

"Shit, shit, shit." He was nervous now. As if he had just checked himself in for surgery, or as if he'd walked himself down death row by choice.

There was a light tapping from the roof above him, and Kiddo peered up at the flaky paint of the shelter's ceiling.

So that was where Dom was. Laid out flat, and as impossible to see as Kiddo was impossible to miss.

He gripped the old bench and scuffed his shoes loudly. Agitated.

The air clouded from his mouth with the cold, but his palms were clammy and hot.

When he swallowed, his mouth was dry and he ended up gulping air.

He couldn't talk to Dom in case anyone was watching. But he sure wished he could just get up and lie on that roof too.

He waited for half an hour before headlights shone in the distance. But it was a car more nondescript than Mrs Dorris', and it drove on by.

There was a very light tap on the roof a few minutes later, which made Kiddo still his fidgeting and glance up again.

His eyes caught a faint flicker of movement from the connecting street.

One … no, two wraiths hiding in the shadows. Near invisible.

Kiddo pretended not to see them. He whistled and shifted where he sat – jumpy with too much energy, but trying to appear as if he were attempting to find a warmer position.

He made sure not to react when, out of the corner of his eye, he noted the near invisible wraiths pulling off their masks and standing up.

They walked beside each other as if they had simply been strolling down the street.

"Hey mate," one of them greeted him cheerfully. They both stopped in front of the small shelter, essentially blocking his way out.

He suppressed the urge for fight or flight, remaining seated.

"Hey," Kiddo nodded a greeting.

"You're not from The Lair, are you?" the second one asked with a friendly tone.

"Yep," Kiddo answered somewhat stiffly. "One of Hato's. I needed a break."

"One of Hato's," the first whistled between his teeth. "I can see you might need a break from that one. He would rule with a tight fist."

"You club regulars?" Kiddo tried to make false conversation.

"Sure," the second one smiled. "Just came from there now."

"You know, the bus doesn't come this late," first one said, and he twisted a ring on his finger so that it was the right way up.

It had a rather sharp point to it. As if he'd just removed its stone.

"But we're getting picked up from here in a minute, if you need a ride."

He twisted it again, and the sharp side of the ring was hidden.

Kiddo heard, and then saw the approaching van.

He couldn't just go with them. He needed to give Dom an in. Which meant he needed more of them to pile out.

He cringed inwardly. It was all happening now. No going back.

"Thanks, but I prefer not to."

"Oh sure," the second guy answered smoothly. "We get it. Hato would have told you never to trust strangers," he teased a little.

"Something like that," Kiddo grunted.

"Well, no hard feelings," the first held his hand out. Sly.

Dying inside, Kiddo shook the first guy's hand, and

watched as the snatcher made it a very hearty shake – closing the other hand, with the sharp edged, downturned ring, over Kiddo's.

Kiddo winced at the sting, and glared at the guy.

"Sorry," the guy said unapologetically, as the van's breaks were slammed on and more wraiths poured out.

The two guys were already pulling their masks back on, and Kiddo found himself hemmed in by five of them.

"Oh lordy, would you look at this one," someone commented.

"He's like … an eleven." There was a fascinated pause. "That's crazy. I've never seen one."

"It's never been a thing."

Kiddo pushed himself up from the bench and made to charge at them, to cause a scene, but he found himself already lurching on his feet.

One incredibly big snatcher caught him before he fell, and gripped Kiddo's arms hard.

"So we got the one the fuss has been about," the snatcher commented. "And he's one of Hato's." There was a chuckle from under the bleeding fangs of the mask, before the snatcher took a handful of Kiddo's shirt and shook him.

A ripping sound told Kiddo he'd just lost his first two buttons.

"You know Hato and your crew are responsible for the most snatcher deaths in this whole city?" the snatcher spat.

"That's good," Kiddo slurred. He probably seemed spaced out, peering over the guy's shoulder. But he had just seen a sixth snatcher jump lightly down out of the shadows to add himself subtly to their ranks.

"I nearly killed Hato last week," the snatcher gloated into Kiddo's face.

"Didn't though," Kiddo pointed out, grinning lopsidedly. His legs were totally gone from underneath him now. He was counting on the oaf to hold him up.

"If you're one of his," the guy hissed. "This will kill him more."

On the other hand, *they* didn't know or care enough about each other to realise that Dom wasn't one of theirs. Kiddo chuckled to himself and shook his head.

"Idiots," Kiddo informed them dopily. "So silly."

The big guy kept his grip on Kiddo's shirt with one hand, but drew back to aim a massive, open handed slap that would hit Kiddo into next year.

"Stand down," a cold voice ordered. And though Dom *wasn't* one of theirs, the authority in his voice automatically made them listen. He had wrapped a tight grip around the big guy's arms. "This one here is going to be our winner. Leave no marks."

"Fine," big guy uttered. "He's the meal ticket."

Someone came forward to zip tie Kiddo's wrists. So they were still doing that old trick. And then he was lugged bodily across to the van, and dumped unceremoniously on its hard floor.

The six snatchers packed into the back of the van after him, hemming Kid in on benches fixed either side of him.

Kiddo tried not to let his eyes roll back. He couldn't stand the idea of passing out and not knowing what was happening to him.

"There's some old bruising on him," a female voice observed, and he felt cold hands roughly pull the ripped part of his shirt aside. "But nothing makeup can't fix."

"I just can't get over his face," someone scoffed. "This guy's gonna knock the competition out of the water. We might as well dump our backup contestants in the bay after seeing this one."

"I can't get over the fact that he's *still* moving around!" the big snatcher growled. An oaf sized boot pressed against Kiddo's kneecap so that it stilled – pinned to the floor. "Go to sleep already!"

"One more rough move with our meal ticket, and I'll give *you* a mark you won't live to regret," Dom's voice said icily.

The snatcher with the fingerless leather-grip gloves. Focus on him.

The boot was removed from Kiddo's knee.

"They dope the contestants before they're first put in the showroom anyway. Mellows them out. The judges won't see any weird ticks or behaviours," someone shrugged off any concern.

"You sure you dosed him right?"

"Maybe I need a new spring put into the injector for the ring."

Nope, Kiddo thought. The spring had packed quite the punch – literally hole punching his skin.

The zip ties were cutting into Kiddo's wrists.

The drug in his system was trying to weight down his eyelids and limbs, while at the same time driving his heart to convulsions. He couldn't stop writhing.

His normal medication probably didn't like whatever they'd given him.

The van stopped momentarily and Kiddo blinked to try to clear his head.

The snatcher with the fingerless gloves was gripping the bench very tightly.

Kiddo's body slid forward a little as the van angled downward. Driving down a ramp for a length of time.

Kiddo started when the van levelled out and stopped.

He felt the big guy's mammoth grip seize the back of his neck to force him upright, and then he was being hauled out like a rag doll.

They were in a giant underground tunnel – like one of those underwater highway passes. There were a number of parked vans.

"Let's see."

Someone pulled his head back by his hair so that his face could be checked.

"Oh my."

He squinted up against the lights foggily.

"The Top Two are going to want to see this. Get them to meet him in the clinic."

A hood was pulled over his head.

Kiddo couldn't help but phase out for what he'd thought was a second, but he gaped when his head lolled sharply as the hood was pulled off again, and he found himself being dragged into a sterile, lab-type room, equipped with a silver topped bench.

He was laid out on the bench under a light, like a body ready for autopsy.

They got rid of his ties – he wasn't even fighting back by twitching anymore.

A nurse had come forward with surgical scissors, snipping her way up his sleeves and then up the middle of his shirt, making both his already popped and his still functional buttons obsolete as she pulled the material away.

Kiddo managed to turn his head back toward the door. The snatchers had all started pulling their masks off. One had his startling blue eyes locked on Kiddo, and the others had still not thought twice about the sixth snatcher's presence.

"Wait out here for when he needs to be moved," a balding doctor instructed, blocking Kiddo's view of Dom.

"Right, we're here. What have we got?"

A short, homely woman, middle aged, swept in. She carried herself like royalty.

She was followed by a taller man, older, who also appeared to run the show. He had an air of hostile confidence.

The Top Two reigning snatchers of the capital.

"My God," the man uttered. "We've won."

The woman swept forward and took a sharp hold of Kiddo's face, turning it up to the light so she could examine it.

The nurse had started on Kiddo's pants, and he heard the doctor close the door. Shutting him in. Shutting Dom out.

Kiddo saw a calculating smile curve the lips of the woman's unremarkable mouth.

"Nearly symmetrical features," the doctor observed, placing a cold, steel ruler to divide the sides of Kiddo's face.

"Healthy head of hair," the woman commented.

"Yes madam," the doctor agreed.

"But get a groomer down here. I want to get a lot of it off his face," the man mused. He was really nothing special either.

Kiddo wasn't sure why the lacklustre appearance of the capital's reigning snatchers was vaguely disappointing.

"Of course, sir." The nurse moved to a telephone at once.

"Clear eyes – hazel. That's always a crowd pleaser. Good teeth," the doctor moved about the bench, prodding and pulling at Kiddo.

He even measured the lengths of Kiddo's arms and legs to make sure they matched. "Good height, good width," he announced. "Good muscle mass."

The nurse came back to finish the job, making a few neat snips with the cool scissor blades moving against the skin of Kiddo's thighs until she could pull his underwear away.

"Oh yes, good everything," the 'madam' noted. "This is absolutely going to make our fortune."

"Our empire," the man agreed. "It was a level playing field before. But you can't argue with this."

The doctor and nurse took hold of Kiddo's limbs and rolled him over.

"Outwardly very fit," the doctor was saying. "They won't be able to take marks off for physique."

"There's a freckle on the back of his right thigh," the nurse tsked.

"No matter," 'sir' said. "It doesn't detract."

Kiddo was rolled back.

"The snatchers outside said he seemed to have all of his mental faculties too, but commented that it took the drugs a while to deaden his twitching," the doctor told the Top Two then.

"Hmm. Tourette's possibly? We'll mask it with something."

"He's still looking at us with such clarity," the madam remarked. "Must be strong willed to be fighting the sleep."

Fingers clicked above Kiddo's nose.

"Hi there!" sir enunciated loudly. "Have you got anything else wrong with you?"

"Pay attention!" madam slapped at Kiddo's cheeks. "Are you faulty in any other way? It won't be good for you to lie."

Kiddo made a groggy decision.

He flopped his head slowly, with great effort, from side to side. No other faults.

"Got any special skills?" sir asked then.

Another barely lucid decision.

"Dance ..." Kiddo could hardly utter the words. "Neon light dance ... Lots of ... flashing."

"Ooooh, I've seen those on the internet," madam hissed with enthusiasm. "Imagine how wild the judges would go if his stage moment was a light show. We could get glow paints to define his muscles and hide his bruises. Strobe lights ..."

Sir was nodding. "I can imagine it. Spectacular."

The nurse was dragging a pair of loose fitting pants up Kiddo's legs, finally tying the drawstrings to keep them in place.

"You better start thinking up a good routine now," madam instructed Kiddo. "Flips, twirls, the lot. It'll be the one time you're unchained while you're here, so live it up."

The door opened and closed again. The groomer had arrived.

"Oh, *perfect*," a deep voice approved, and a brawny bearded man hovered into view. He clicked open a briefcase.

"Yes, we want less hair obscuring the perfect face. Keep some length at the top though," madam ordered. "We want them to see he won't go the way of the doctor over here." She glanced at the doctor's bald spot with distaste.

"And do a sharper cut on the back and sides," sir put in. "Make it edgy."

The doctor helped to lever and hold Kiddo in an upright position as the groomer began buzzing around him.

Kiddo, even with his vision whirling and his head stuffed with clouds, resented the fact that he was slumped over this disgusting excuse for a health professional, being held by him.

Nothing like Frazzle, who had grown up in a warzone and still become a saint of a person.

Kid felt a smooth metal loop close around one ankle then. And the other. Two more were added to his wrists. Another around his throat, as if he was being put into a collar.

They felt thick. Like cuffs. And the nurse busily started connecting each of them with short chains that would mean he could hardly lift his arms or shuffle his steps.

"It was worth ordering the fancier sets for this," madam approved. "The titanium cuffs will look great under the strobe lights."

The groomer finished up and winked at Kiddo. "Pays to have a pretty face."

"Pays us anyway," sir said. "And more than a pretty face. We have a whole new, wealthier future to plan out ahead of us."

"Not even counting what we'll get for the other normal tens we collected." Madam headed the way to the door, sir disappearing after her, and the groomer following.

"Move him," the doctor instructed the snatchers waiting outside. "By tomorrow you will have all been transferred more digits than you've ever seen for tonight's efforts."

The nurse tied a blindfold over Kiddo's eyes.

He felt the meaty grip of the oaf on one side, and a firm, but more supportive grip on the other.

He still couldn't support himself, and had to let himself be pulled along on the journey to wherever the holding cells were.

His bare feet dragged along smooth, cool floors as his head hung down against his chest with exhaustion.

He was hardly ready for it when they stopped. There was the feel of air being moved – a door being opened, and his blindfold was dragged away so that his eyes smarted and burned against the incredibly white lights.

"I'll do it," Dom spoke to the burly, sour snatcher firmly. "You'll probably break him tossing him in."

The oaf dropped his hold, throwing his hands up, and strode off with a scowl.

Dom caught and held Kiddo against himself and walked him into the cell, lowering him carefully.

The whole time Kiddo could hear Dom whispering to him, softly, beside his ear.

"You're ok. I've got you. You're ok. I'll work this place out. We'll get out."

"I'm fine," Kiddo managed to slur just as quietly.

"It's ok to sleep now," Dom whispered. Kiddo felt Dom's

exposed fingertips against the soft bristles of his new haircut as Dom gently lowered Kiddo's head to a soft floor. "Rest now. Now it's my turn to go to work."

Kiddo felt Dom reluctantly withdraw. The rush of air as the door closed.

He couldn't even curl up to comfort himself. But stayed laid out as he'd been placed.

"You'd be a tender lover," one of the other snatchers joked to Dom mockingly.

"I bet if I looked like that, people would treat me gentle too," someone else griped. "Heck, that kid's even making *me* question my sexuality. But after tonight, maybe I'll be able afford to buy one of those tens myself."

"Personally, I think I'd be buying Honolulu."

"No way, imagine a night with Rome."

Their voices faded. But they were not replaced by silence.

Kiddo passed out at last to the sounds of faint cries from all the other competitors he couldn't lift his head to see.

| 27 |

Twenty Seven

Kiddo was certain he would lose his mind.

The constant white lights were driving him nuts.

The staggered arrival of three different nourishing meals, and the fact that he wasn't starving between them, told him that only one day must have passed in this monotony. But it felt like it could have been a week.

His teachers would be rolling their eyes right out of their heads if that was the case.

Just as bad was the fact that there wasn't enough room to pace his cell – it was the size of a very small walk-in closet. And his chains made it into barely a shuffle anyway.

Being one of the last free, Kiddo's cell was an uncomfortably curved 'corner' cell where the aisle made a bend toward the front guard area. However it gave him a view where, on the right angles, he could see into his left neighbour's cell a little, and he could also see more of the long aisle than just the competitors across from him.

His neighbour was stunning, and had given him a cheeky smile the first time Kiddo had found that angle. A wink the second time Kiddo had paced. And a sexy air kiss the next time.

The young man had the most luscious eyelashes Kiddo had ever seen – which he batted like weapons. His cheekbones could have cut butter, and his lips were full and sensual. His face and skull were stubbled, though mixed with the touches of femininity, it was a striking look.

All of the other competitors in view gave Kiddo a much clearer understanding of what being a ten meant – with breathtaking displays of masculine, feminine and androgynous beauty on display. There were beauties from all over the world, of every shape, size and colour. But any time any of them tried to communicate, snatchers came in and threats were made that shut them up.

When he'd first woken properly, Kiddo had become certain that there was no way Dom would be able to visit him again without giving them away. He'd given up watching, and the only other thing he could do, was lay with his hands on his stomach, kicking his legs into the padded walls to get rid of energy.

Kicking his legs into the glass, even if unbreakable, always got him yelled at.

At all times there was someone watching the many cells from a computer at a desk near the door. The snatcher guard could also easily wander up and down the cells and see absolutely everything the tens could be doing wrong at any time too.

Sighing loudly in frustration as he stared at the white roof, Kiddo was just about to start punching the cushy floor when he heard a familiar voice.

"Hey bud, want a mint?"

Kiddo rolled onto his stomach and levered himself up in time to see a snatcher swiping a wafer-thin mint strip from Dom. The snatcher shoved Dom's shoulder.

"Out of my face."

"Good idea," Dom nodded, stepping back as the snatcher snavelled the mint into his mouth.

There was a moment of refreshment for the unhappy snatcher, before his head popped. With a bang. Like a balloon bursting.

"Huh," Dom said as the body dropped, and then he stepped over it to get to Kiddo's cell.

He knelt at Kiddo's air vent and spoke too quietly for any of the other caged contestants to hear. And almost too quickly for Kiddo to catch.

"I've been all over. They have a convention centre space. Pretty grand. You'll all be set up at your own booths for pre-judging. Then those who qualify will have their own moment to shine on stage."

Dom was jabbing his finger into Kiddo's glass and frowning as if he were delivering demands instead of information.

"I think the stage show will be the best time for the gang to strike. I know you'll be selected."

Jab.

"Itinerary says two in the afternoon for the show."

Jab, jab, jab.

"The audience will be at capacity. Everyone will want to be watching. Seems like you've been tagged on last."

Exasperated rather than angry expression for a moment.

"But of course, there's no cell phone reception down here.

In a minute I'll use this computer. I'll send everything through to the others."

"Don't get caught," Kiddo told him. "Tell the others that my performance will be the perfect distraction for them to come in on."

"Ok," Dom accepted that with a curt nod.

He glanced around, scowling at any watchers.

"You good?" Dom asked then, with more longing than he'd let himself show before.

"All good. No fear."

"None?" Dom grimaced. But then he stood briskly.

"Make sure you know your routine," he growled loudly at Kiddo. "You *better* get it right."

He rounded on the other contestants then. "And if anyone opens their mouth about all this," he announced loudly, "I'll blow your head off too. I've bet every dollar on this one to win." He hooked a thumb back at Kiddo. "And I'll happily get rid of any of you."

He definitely gave off a convincingly crazy-killer snatcher vibe.

There were heads being shaken and lips being pressed together.

Nobody was going to say a single thing against him.

He crossed to the computer desk, double checking that all surveillance was directed on the cells, rather than any cameras pointing at the screen.

He turned the monitor so that none of the contestants could see what he was doing either, but as Dom sat at the chair and then started playing with his belt and pants area, it sure looked questionable – and perhaps added to the crazy vibe.

He worked his belt, then the computer, then stood with a smile of satisfaction.

He crossed to a phone anchored to the concrete wall beside the desk and pressed one of the office number buttons.

"Yes, hello," he smiled wolfishly as he put on a panicked voice. "The cell guard has been murdered. I saw one of the foreign snatchers, possibly Russian, do it. I think the reigning snatchers of Moscow were going to try to sabotage the competition! You need to tell our Top Two at once!" he twirled the red curly cord in his fingers. "Ahuh, of course I'll man the post until they get down here. Thank you!"

He hung up and then waggled his fingers at Kiddo. "Remember, you're *my* winner."

Then, not manning the post at all, he left.

Kiddo could feel the eyes of the other contestants on him. But they all remained silent.

Or nearly all.

"I don't think that was all it seemed," an amused voice purred softly from the cell beside his.

Kiddo shot his neighbour a dark, warning look.

So maybe someone *had* heard what they were saying.

His neighbour held up his hands. "Don't shoot," he grinned. "I won't breathe a word."

"You won't if you know what's good for you," Kiddo answered. Blunt, because it was the truth.

"I wouldn't want to take on your lethal friend and get my head popped," his neighbour replied. He was speaking quietly, but there was a masculine husk to his voice, along with a curving, drawn out way of enunciating each word.

"More because I believe you *are his* rather than because I believe he'll kill us all too."

"Best to believe both," Kiddo shrugged.

"Mmmmm," his neighbour nodded slowly. "I've seen the power of true boy love before. I hope it's enough to save rather than kill us all instead."

Kiddo sighed. "I'm Kiddo. Can I truly count on you to keep your mouth shut?"

"Of cooourse," his neighbour smiled a Cheshire smile. "I'm Pash. And I'm only your threat in terms of beauty rankings."

The doors to the room burst open and the first few snatchers nearly skidded and slipped over in the muck that had been left on the floor from the guard.

Kiddo sank back down in his cell, somewhat bolstered by the fact that Dom could still be so Dom in this place ... and by the intense arguments and accusations that started flying as snatchers from all different backgrounds arrived to check on their goods.

| 28 |

Twenty Eight

One by one the contestants were taken from their cells and blindfolded.

But first, they were swamped by three snatchers each.

The process was the same each time – one snatcher to lean on the chain linking a contestant's wrists, another to hold down the shoulders, and the last to smother the contestant's nose until they opened their mouth and could be dosed with something to make them docile.

Pash sneered and spat, but then was gone.

The cells around him emptied.

Kiddo sat cross legged on his padded floor, legs bouncing and fingers tapping on his knee as he waited for his turn.

He'd been last in, and was last out.

"We bought you something special," the snatchers told him as they opened his door and pounced on him. "To tone down those fidgets."

He glared up at them, first suffocating on a hand, and then choking on whatever they pushed down his gullet.

"This'll have you niiiice and calm."

The blinding lights were replaced by the darkness of a blindfold.

He half staggered on his chains as they dragged him up and out of the cell.

He knew he'd reached a washroom before they took the blindfold off by the feel of the steam and heat that misted against his skin.

The cuffs stayed on, but his ankles were unlinked, and the blindfold and ridiculously thin pants were off immediately before he slipped as they pushed him under the harsh jets of water.

He gritted his teeth as he was scrubbed to within an inch of his life, and then was dried so briskly and thoroughly that he was at risk of losing all of his features.

But, as promised, he was starting to find it hard to care.

The usual tension that heightened him to a point of constant, restless movement had for once melted away.

It was kind of nice.

His eyes were covered and his ankles were linked again, but it was fine, because they were taking him where he needed to be and he didn't have to be the one trying to get there on time or trying to remember everything.

"This is his exhibition stand," someone said, and his body was yanked toward the voice. "You can connect up his chains to those loops so he doesn't relax too much."

He felt himself get pushed up a very slight step, his feet on a smooth surface, like a shower floor.

There was the tinkling sound of chains, and his blindfold was removed so that he could see he was in a sort of pod, or stand. As if he were a doll in its box.

Just like a doll with the wire twisters keeping its limbs in place, they connected his neck cuff to a short length of titanium links that locked onto a loop at about shoulder height. His ankles were connected to another loop on the floor.

It would give him the ability to turn a little, but not to sit down or step down out of the pod. That was alright – he wouldn't have to remember how he was meant to be positioned or what he was meant to be doing.

A girl rushed forward with product to style his hair.

"I want it masterfully tousled," madam's voice drew Kiddo's flimsy thread of attention then. She'd put on a coating of makeup and a long gown for the occasion.

"Angle the lights low to show off those cheekbones and abs," sir added. He was suited up.

But still, neither were impressive.

Madam slapped at the girl – a groomer. "I said *masterfully.* Effortlessly, carefully placed."

That didn't make sense.

"Y-yes, madam."

Maybe it did?

Kiddo didn't mind. He didn't have to be the one messing up or getting jumbled this time. How lovely.

The groomer started dabbing a sponge with makeup over Kiddo's still healing chest and rib bruises. It was cold, and Kiddo broke out with goosebumps at once.

"I could just eat him up." Sir did little fist pumps in the air. Celebrating.

"Whoever buys him just might," madam shrugged. "Some

people believe you are what you consume. Beauty is no different."

A techy was at Kiddo's feet, twisting and angling some little white spotlights, but when Kiddo peered down at their glaring beams, they made his vision funny.

Uh oh.

It was never good when his vision went funny.

But it was just so damn hard to care.

"What colour globes would please the Top Two?" the techy asked, opening a hip bag with pinks, blues, golds ... so many colour options.

"We could go for glory and pick gold," sir rubbed his hands together now.

"And let the light take away from his tone?" madam frowned at sir as if he were an idiot. "No, we need something neutral and natural to go with cool-beige skin."

The techy got to work making it happen, adjusting the strength of the spotlights so that some were softer and some were brighter, until the light illuminating Kiddo's body was like that of a fresh, autumn morning, where the sun is silvery and pale.

"We'll be seated in the arena later," madam turned to the groomer, who was now neatening Kiddo's nails. "You'll have to come straight over when the judging's done here, and get to work on his body paint. I want it to be fierce. Like a warrior's paint. And make those muscles glow."

"Yes madam."

"And you won't have long before he's wriggling with energy," sir warned. "We'll be sending over some high performance drugs, stronger than top athletes would touch, to wake him back up for the performance."

"Yes sir."

"Give him a few sips of water, but not enough to bloat him," sir added.

The girl hurried to unscrew the cap off a bottle of water on her trolley. She pressed a straw to Kiddo's mouth and he drank obediently.

"Enough." Madam roughly moved Kiddo to stand straighter, peering at his face and body sharply. "Beautiful," she approved.

"Atlanta and Tokyo have given their contestant's nicknames on introductory plaques," sir observed. "Should we do the same?"

Kiddo noticed dimly that Pash was a distance away. His sign announced that he was from Sydney, Australia.

Madam pursed her lips. "What would we call him?"

Sir tapped his chin.

Kiddo smiled giddily. "I'm Raze."

Madam turned back to Kiddo with a hiss, ready to strike. Then she scowled. "You wish."

Kiddo tilted his head. "We're all Raze. Coming to get you."

Sir stepped very close to Kiddo's face, and spoke intensely – forcing Kiddo to hold most of his wandering attention on the man.

"You might have heard some hero tales. But nobody is coming to save you. Do not say that name again."

"Forget the name idea altogether," madam dismissed it all, turning to leave. "He's just a beautiful idiot. An identity is not necessary."

Sir nodded, stepping back. "Time to mingle with potential buyers for the beautiful idiot then."

"*Lucky* idiot," the groomer girl sniped at Kiddo under her breath as the Top Two walked away. "Just having to stand there and be pretty." She pinched him meanly with a pair of tweezers, but he was incredibly slow to react.

"I don't think I'd want to be in his place," the techy grinned. "Who knows what a buyer might want to do to flesh like that?"

The groomer cheered up a little then. She began packing up her kit. "Who knows the kind of fetishes they might be into."

She wheeled her kit away, smirking over her shoulder at Kiddo as the techy joined her.

"Raze will get you," Kiddo murmured back, hardly knowing what he was saying.

He was still totally unbothered by anything in the world.

All of the contestants were in their own doll boxes. Pretty little pods with lights.

All wearing silver-grey shorts or two-pieces.

"Lordy, those shorts don't leave much to the imagination," a quiet, good natured voice came from a masked snatcher, who had just stopped to post himself as Kiddo's guard. "Wowee."

He was wearing fingerless leather gloves.

"Raaaaaaze," Kiddo nearly strangled himself as he tried to take a step forward and was yanked backward. "Told em. They didn't believe."

"Easy there," Dom quickly helped Kiddo regain his balance before resuming his post. "Don't want you to hang yourself."

"I'm fine. S'nice not to be worried about anything," Kiddo told him. "Numb is peaceful."

Dom was watching forward, his arms by his sides like a soldier. Every competitor had a guard like him. But Dom looked particularly stiff.

"How 'bout you?" Kiddo asked politely. "You seem tense."

Dom shifted slightly. "I guess numb might be nice. But I'm watching for the other Razes. They're not meant to do anything drastic until you said – your spectacular stage performance. Though you never know, if one of them gets found out, we could have a problem."

"Oh, they'll know when I'm up, it's going to be really something," Kiddo chuckled. It was like he could already feel the abnormal electrical impulses starting to spike in his brain.

The hazy euphoria could have been the drugs, or another symptom.

And the whole place – which Kiddo only now noticed was absolutely huge, lined with the pods at the back where the spectators were starting to enter, and then opening out to an arena of plush spectating chairs that faced an expansive concert stage … all of it had a kind of … aura around it. Unreal.

But he just couldn't find it within himself to care.

"They're all gorgeous, I can hardly choose who to bid on," a passer-by gushed to her friend as they entered the walkway through the pods.

"I thought you wanted to start collecting ivory ones again," the woman's friend asked. "Redo some of the earlier shades you hung up on your wall."

"Gah! I know, but look at them all! Imagine that one's head in the top right corner."

"It's not the right shade, it'll be too stark beside the Singaporean head."

Pash was the 'it' they were referring to. He had the deep, rich shade of skin that Velvet had.

"But it's so pretty!"

"Let's just focus on who to bet on," the woman's friend patted her hand. "Go for the win."

These two were clearly not reigning snatchers. They were the buyers. The people who harvested other human beings for nefarious purposes.

They were lovely in their expensive gowns, and Kiddo smiled at them dumbly as they gasped and stopped at his stand.

"This one's got to be the winner," the first one, with the trophy wall at home, stated. "Imagine how this one would look."

They stepped in as close as they could, scanning every bit of Kiddo before Dom cleared his throat.

"No touching the merchandise unless you've bought it," Dom told them flatly.

They hmphed, but turned at once and hurried over to a snatcher stand for taking bets.

A group of four men paused on the way to their seats next, eyeing Kiddo with interest.

"East Asian descent, do you think?" one of the group members asked curiously. "I wonder if he was originally from this area or if they shipped him in. I'm quite sure that's against the rules."

"He has hazel in his eyes," another responded. His white gloves were so bright in the spotlights, they filled Kiddo's vision. "Is that usual for that region?"

"Very interesting."

"He's going to be costly."

"No matter," the first one said. "If the price is right, we can collect him. And it will be worth it."

"Please sirs," Dom gestured to how the concert lights were lowering, but his voice was a bit growly. "It's time to find your seats."

Then the judges arrived, and all Dom could do was cross his arms and stay quiet.

They had tape measures, magnifying glasses, stethoscopes, little torches to shine into his pupils – which really didn't help that aura of swirling mist in Kiddo's eyes.

It tasted like Kiddo had been sucking on some old keys and the lock to go with them.

"Full points and even bonus points for build and features," one of them murmured.

"This is like a miracle," another whispered in a low voice, aghast.

"Like we need a whole new classification."

They gestured for a nurse to come forward. They were going to test some of his inner aesthetics too.

She drew blood, dividing it up and setting the tubes into a machine on wheels. She held up a scanner that she roamed over his body. She checked his teeth. She tapped him in different places. She even cupped him in different places.

He just blinked like a doped-up dope.

"Very dilatated pupils, but it makes sense under the circumstances. Blood work is clear of any nasties, other than whatever drugs they laced him with. His organs are strong. His muscles look good. He is a healthy specimen on the inside," the nurse affirmed.

The doctors on the surface had never seen his epilepsy show up in an MRI either … but it was there. And it was just waiting for its turn with the strobe lights … For once one of his complex focal seizures was going to be welcome. He hoped it made him scream, rant, run around or wreck his loose shorts with something real surprising for them.

Kiddo gave a chuckle.

Then he couldn't remember why he was chuckling.

How odd.

"Check his mind, as best you can in this state," one of the judges said, pressing his hands against Kiddo's chest to test for firmness.

Another judge was checking how smooth his skin felt, running clinical fingers over his outer thigh.

"Young man," the nurse snapped her fingers in front of his face. "Tell me what you are thinking at this moment."

Kiddo strained for a thought.

There was one!

"You have very advanced medical equipment, ma'am," he answered. "It could be helpful to share on the surface."

"Beautiful ethical nature, and good manners," one of the judges gave two very definite ticks on their clip board.

"What else is on your mind?" the nurse pushed.

Gosh. What else was on his mind?

Dom. Oh, and Sparks. All the other Razes on their way. What were they going to do?

Feed Duncan Jr. Don't miss the bus. Fold the washing.

He'd nearly forgotten!

"I need to remember to take summary notes for the chemistry test. I need to write a plan for an essay question, and include quotes. I've got to answer the equations for exercise seven. I should revise the history of the United Nations and its policies on human rights – which is quite relevant, isn't it? And I've got to read pages eight to twelve of my 'Modern World Legal' text. If I forget, I won't stay top of my classes," he told the nurse seriously.

"Educated." Another two big ticks followed. "Hard working. Excelling."

"Where did they get this kid?" one of the judges questioned in disbelief. "They better still be selecting from nobodies. We don't need the law to start caring."

"Do you have parents?" the nurse asked, giving Kiddo a shake as his eyes wandered off.

The lights were getting even lower. The aura was getting more noticeable.

The stage was being set and beautifully gowned buyers and reigning snatchers were taking their seats.

"I really wouldn't know, ma'am," Kiddo admitted genuinely. "I might have forgotten them on the streets."

"Street kid," a judge said in relief. "Nobody."

None of them noticed the snatcher in the fingerless gloves, bunching his fists. Controlling himself.

Kiddo smiled.

"Such a dazzling smile," one of them added then. "I think we have all we need for this part of the judging."

With a few final glances and disbelieving head shakes, the

judges and nurse left the pod section and headed down the countless aisles to get to the front, where they would view the stage performances next.

The groomer girl came rushing back with a few other masked snatchers on her heels, each of them with harried movements as they quickly opened their kits.

He'd been last to be seen by the judges, and every other contestant was already either finished or nearly done being made over.

Pash was in a jaw dropping, floor length gold dress that glittered in Kiddo's eyes, even from all the way over there.

The first contestant was up on stage. She was literally up there, singing for her life.

"Get those drugs into him quick-smart!" the original groomer girl ordered. "We need him alert for this next bit!"

Two snatchers forced Kiddo unnecessarily against the back of the pod, driving three pills down his throat and washing them down with splashes of water.

"*Careful!*" the groomer girl snarled as Kiddo spluttered. "You'll make the paint run!"

She'd already started painting glow in the dark forks of lightning across his skin.

Not as nice as a lotus lagoon.

The second performance was up – dramatic music was playing, but this competitor appeared to be shooting flaming arrows. Of course, a masked snatcher stood with a gun poised to kill should the contestant try anything against the crowd.

Kiddo shivered as the groomers accosted him with paint

now, and he grimaced as something inside him seemed to click jarringly, and then lurch.

Where there had been looseness to his muscles and brain, now there was growing energy and adrenaline.

Ticking, tightening, buzzing.

Ah, *there* were all those worries and fidgets.

"Oh God," Kiddo groaned, half falling back against the pod wall.

"Don't you dare!" the original groomer girl threatened, and one of the snatchers stopped him from wrecking her work.

"What did you give him?" Dom asked.

"Hold his damn leg still!" the groomer girl demanded.

"You didn't overdose him, did you?" Dom again.

"Why do you care?" she had moved on to Kiddo's face now. She gripped his head like a vice. "Don't let him clutch his chest like that! It'll smudge!"

"The Top Two will sure care," Dom growled.

"I just fed him whatever the Top Two themselves sent down," she snapped. "So if they kill him it's their own fault."

"They wouldn't kill him," another snatcher shrugged. "He's gonna be our money-maker."

The whirring of hair dryers and the hot air stole Kiddo's breath away as he was suddenly surrounded in them.

"Right, he's dry. We're done."

The original girl loosened Kiddo's chains so that he could sit down.

"Don't pass out or wreck your paint, or madam will skin you."

They packed up. They didn't give him a second glance, but wheeled off to get a good spot to see the show.

A third performer was juggling knives.

"Shit … shit … shit," Kiddo was still grimacing.

"Kiddo? What exactly are you feeling like now?"

Kiddo's breaths were coming fast.

"Ah man," Kiddo winced, pressing his hand to his sternum.

"Ah man," Dom repeated. Worry colouring his voice as he tried not to look like a caring guard while at the same time wanting to be a caring guard.

"You know how I said numb …" Kiddo took a deep breath. "Was peaceful?"

"Yeah?"

"This is the opposite."

Kiddo put his hands on either side of his pod and lowered himself down so that he wouldn't fall.

"Oh dear," Dom stated.

Kiddo groaned, leaning his head back against the cool pod wall.

"The guy who was meant to be on duty here had the job of getting you backstage when it's time," Dom said hurriedly. "I have a key for your chains. I can get you out of here if you need me to, right now."

Kiddo was gasping fast breaths in, but gave Dom a lopsided smile.

"Do you have a key for anywhere else?"

Dom's blue eyes were keen, standing out from the grotesque mask. "No, but I've been doing great just slipping around when there are convenient openings."

"There won't be any convenient slipping about with a guy covered in glow in the dark fluoro paint," Kiddo told him.

He took handfuls of his masterfully, carefully effortless hair and held his head.

It was pulsing. Ready to pop, like that snatcher Dom had given a wafer mint to.

"Did … did the snatcher who was meant to be guarding me need a mint too?" Kiddo asked.

"Actually," Dom answered. "He needed a neck adjustment."

The first few contestants were led back to their pods while contestant five was up there reading a poem.

Dom and Kiddo kept quiet as the snatcher guards of the next few contestants unhooked their charges and took them away.

"My heart is trying to jump out of my chest," Kiddo said when they were gone. "It feels like every bit of caffeine and sugar I've avoided for the last few years, every kind of wake-me-up drug I ever took as a kid, and every single ADHD spark in my body has fired up to party."

The palpitations were driving him wild. He was exploding from every pulse point in his body.

"This has got to be what a heart attack feels like."

"Please don't die on me," Dom said anxiously.

"Distract me then, before I burst," Kiddo wheezed.

"Okay. Well, there's some bad news," Dom told him quickly, eyes on the stage, where a competitor was performing a ballet solo.

"Great."

"Bad news is, there are one hundred and ninety-five capitals in the world," Dom said.

"Ohhh great," Kiddo moaned. "One hundred and ninety-five performances to get through. I'm the signal to our Raze gang, and I'm last."

"No, no. Time is precious to these people. Only the top forty favourites are chosen to perform, and they've got a maximum of two minutes each, with very short transition times," Dom supplied. "So, about eighty minutes all up, and we're already up to the seventh competitor."

"How do you know I was even chosen?" Kiddo asked, winded by pangs in his stomach and chest.

"It was never in question," Dom told him. "But," he pointed at a number of other pods, where the spotlights had been turned off the competitors. "They light up their stars."

Kiddo's lights were on as bright as ever.

"Turns out," Kiddo grunted. "Snatchers run a pretty tight show."

"Well oiled," Dom agreed. "Oily bastards."

"None of the snatcher empire would work if there wasn't a market of buyers in the first place," Kiddo glowered.

"Hey, there's some good news to distract you with," Dom reassured him. "I got into another computer room last night. Made it nice and private so I could focus –"

"Oh?"

"That one was another four mints," Dom explained. "Messy, messy. But I installed a hidden screen share, remote controller app and contacted Jingle and Trix. They got their hacker magic on. And, boy, did they go *deep*."

"How deep?" Kiddo's palms were clammy, but rubbing them on his barely there shorts didn't help.

"Jingle found an encrypted dark web file." Kiddo could tell Dom was grinning as he said this. "A shared file used by the reigning snatchers of each capital."

"But snatchers, and especially reigning snatchers, have no surface identity."

"Yet their buyers *do*."

Kiddo held his breath for a moment. Frowning. "They wouldn't be so stupid as to use their real names."

"Of course not," Dom agreed. "But we all leave enough data in the world that a talented hacker can work out a trail. You put together payments, orders, passwords, messages, locations … you eventually crack the code. Jingle made an algorithm to do it for her."

"She … has the buyer files?"

"She has the buyer files," Dom affirmed.

The next lot of competitors were brought back and another batch taken.

"Not only that," Dom whispered now – the next performance was a piano piece, which was less noisy than others had been. "But she has turned those files in to the police."

"The *police*?" Kiddo guffawed. They had never got involved before. Not with the root of the problem behind any disappearances. They'd never gone deeper to connect the disappearances, because they themselves were trapped by the corrupt system and leaders too.

But, they *had* known pretty well what Hato and the gang

was always up to, and had made an effort to keep the heat off The Lair.

"Or should I say, the police, the intelligence services and the public news stations of every capital in the world," Dom corrected. "Any corrupt buyer in the world who hasn't come to die at this event is going to have their name dragged through the mud and be ruined anyway."

Kiddo straightened his spine a little, trying not to hyper-ventilate.

The stars were really sparking in his eyes now. As if he could see the sizzling wires of his brain as they started to short circuit.

"The law would never be able to turn on all these people. They're protected by their money and power," Kiddo man-aged. "It'll be suppressed."

His muscles were spasming.

"Maybe the system is broken, or stuck," Dom said. "But the majority of the public and people who work for the law are not. As soon as even a hint of something like this is picked up on by the first relatively good cop or person on the web, this will spread like wildfire. The names of the buyers will be everywhere, and they will be hated and destroyed. Social media, regular media, and finally the system will be swamped with the truth."

"That …" Kiddo acquiesced, "is pretty good news."

"That is world changing," Dom answered with satisfac-tion. "No matter what happens today, no matter if we fail in razing the snatchers here – we've still hurt them beyond repair. They have been breached, they aren't able to protect their buyers. And their buyers are dead meat."

"Do you … happen to know what the plan is today?"

Dom eyed the next contestant – a belly dancer.

"As we speak, if all went well," Dom explained, "Flip, Seethe, Start and Trix will be rolling mini grenades down opportune hallways and stations. Anywhere snatchers might still be if they didn't come to the expo."

"That would be," Kiddo drew in a breath. "A massive job, surely?"

"Yes and no," Dom answered. "I found that the ordinary snatchers, while there is a city's worth of them, have to keep to very set areas. There are very clear precincts of shared sleeping quarters, training squares and rec rooms. But today there's even less of a spread. Everyone was either coming here, or watching the show from screens in the rec areas."

"The rest of our Razes then?" Kiddo questioned.

"Jingle and Sparks were going to try to find a way to access the sound board or light board, or the main control for the stage anyway, so they can take over during your show," Dom paused. "And Hato, Quicklips, Frazzle, Tiny and Velvet are probably working their way around the perimeter of this room right now. All of our Razes will be looking bulky with little grenades lining their pockets, and looking dodgy as they plant some extra things around this whole place to ramp the sound and light show up further."

"How … how on earth did they all manage to get in?" Kiddo half grunted, he was squinting around now, trying to see past the darkness, the swirls from his own brain, and the distance to the perimeter of the room. But there were too many snatchers in too many masks.

"Me," Dom answered. "I'm sorry I wasn't there to try to make things easier for you this morning."

Kiddo raised his eyebrows in amazement. "Maybe you really are a ghost. How have you been able to do all this?"

"Seethe has been collecting plenty of outfits so they could all blend in. I took a van out very early this morning, and picked them up."

"How did you explain the need for the van?" Kiddo asked.

"I used the last of my persuasive mints," he sighed glumly. "And in the chaos, before I slipped into the van and chuffed away, I let everyone know that the French snatchers had been lurking around there, trying to sabotage security and make our area look inept. That pesky Parisian Top Two."

"Thought it was … the Russians. Moscow?"

Dom snickered into his mask. "Since last night, the Brits, the Serbians, the Himalayans, the Cubic Zirconian Capricorns have been absolutely wreaking havoc. I've had to report all of them. Might have to tell madam and sir that I need stress leave."

Kiddo managed a laugh, wincing.

"There were no questions asked when the van idled up to get scanned out, because to get that far up the ramp, you've normally been cleared," Dom went on. "And they were still mopping up the slops from my minty victims when I parked us cosily back in place later on. Nobody took notice of an abundance of lumpy snatchers untangling themselves from the back. Like a clown car, it was."

Dom was trying hard to stay quietly upbeat to distract Kiddo. But he kept turning his head to peer back with worried blue eyes.

"And you wait and see," Dom went on. "Jingle's worked out some way to make the speakers around this whole place transmit the lethal sonic wave. So when you do your distraction, Jingle and Sparks will take over that control box, and in minutes, almost everyone in this room will be dropping on the spot."

The current person on stage was jumping rope, trying to pull out some good tricks. But it seemed like this one's snatchers had been clutching at straws to find their competitor a unique skill to display.

"I'm trying really hard," Kiddo rasped. "Not to accidentally start my distraction right now."

Dom reached back and squeezed Kiddo's ankle, rubbing a thumb hard against his skin, as if he could try to ground Kiddo by the sheer force of will coming from that touch. "Am I allowed to, uh, know? Or is it a surprise?"

"I told them," Kiddo said with effort. "That they should give me a light show. And I would dance."

"Oh dear," Dom uttered, his light tone not concealing the concern. "Not the kind of dance they expect?"

"My limbs will work it out," Kiddo answered through gritted teeth. "And we can blame it on the Viennese, or the Athenians, or anyone at all to cause a stir while the gang make their move."

Dom puffed up his cheeks and blew a big gust of air from under the fang emblem on his mask. "I will set accusations flying from the top of my lungs," he assured Kiddo, giving Kiddo's ankle another squeeze.

They fell silent then.

The next batch of competitors were getting ready to change over.

After them, it would be Kiddo getting unchained and led away.

| 29 |

Twenty Nine

"I've got you, you're alright," Dom was saying under his breath, too quietly for the other snatcher guards to hear as they were tugging their own competitors along by the arms. "They better not have done you lasting damage. But don't you worry…"

To others who might have given them a cursory glance, Dom would have appeared to have been gripping Kiddo's bicep roughly and dragging him along too. But Dom's grip was high up on Kiddo's arm, with both hands almost locked under his armpit so that Kiddo could half lean his weight on that hold like a crutch.

He was counting on Dom to help him stay balanced, even though his ankle chains were no longer connected.

"I almost hope madam and sir *don't* die in the blast," Dom went on saying then. "So I can strangle them myself for the drugs they've given you, let alone everything else. You never know, some people might kick on and need help dying."

It was likely that anyone else would have been successfully bouncing off the walls and ready for a great light show dance after the concoction the Top Two had prescribed Kid. Maybe with some uncomfortable side effects, like a racing heart and the jitters.

But Kiddo had missed out on his regular meds, should not be mixing stimulant amphetamines, was on the lead up to a proper fit, and had been stuffed full of a range of sedatives over the last couple of days that did not seem to be interacting with the more recent pick-me-ups in a friendly manner.

"Feels like I'm having a heart attack," Kiddo admitted in a moan.

"Could just be stage fright?" Dom whispered back hopefully. "You normally prefer to hunch and slouch out of sight."

"I'm not too scared. I think even a seizure could outdo what's going on up there right now," Kiddo murmured.

A competitor was speedily naming all of the countries and capitals of the world by memory. Many people in the crowd were turned to each other in conversation, ignoring the display.

"This one could go over the two minute limit," Dom mused. "But it's interesting."

Kiddo and Dom lost their view of the stage, passing through a door into a nearly completely dark corridor leading to the stage wings. Only a faint blue light, which did not help Kiddo's head, gave away shapes and possible hazards.

Dom moved a little slower then, letting the others pull ahead.

Dom watched the others get further down the corridor, none of them noticing the growing gap at the end of the line.

Kiddo gasped when Dom suddenly swept him against a wall, holding Kiddo up against it with one arm and a bracing leg, before making sure nobody could see them in the shadows.

He quickly ripped up his mask.

"What're you doing?" Kiddo rasped, "I need to go on."

Dom didn't answer, but used his free hand to angle one side of Kiddo's throat cuff down.

Before Kiddo could blink, Dom's lips were on the side of his neck, and Kiddo was melting.

For a moment, Kiddo didn't feel like his whole body was the example of the saying 'storm in a teacup'. Instead, everything was bliss.

He closed his eyes, tilted his head, feeling Dom pressing against him – firm, confident, yearning.

Kissing, nipping at his neck.

Then Dom broke from his neck, roving his hand up along the shaved side of Kiddo's head and lacing kisses up to Kiddo's mouth.

His lips were hot and almost rough against Kiddo's – his tongue insistent, and Kiddo was gasping when Dom drew back.

Dom put a hand on Kiddo's sternum as they both caught their breath.

"Wish I was the only reason for your heart racing that bad," Dom whispered, pulling Kiddo from the wall and against himself in a bear hug, his hand on the titanium cuff at Kiddo's neck.

Kiddo slumped into him, wishing he could just stay like that.

"Don't worry, I didn't mess your paint," Dom said, pulling his mask back down into place.

Kiddo realised that Dom's body covering his was the one thing keeping him from lighting up the whole corridor. But stopping had definitely been a risk, even a worthwhile one.

"I did leave my own mark on you though," Dom snickered, helping Kiddo to get moving again. "Under that neck cuff, that love bite says you're *mine*."

"I thought Sparks is hers, I'm mine and you're your own?" Kiddo panted.

The kisses were still warming the pit of his stomach, but he was tasting metal again and was very close to losing his grip on everything.

"Change of plans," Dom whispered back.

"Where were you?!" a snatcher hissed, in a ferocious mood.

"I got distracted by the countries and capitals competitor," Dom shrugged. "Who knew that the capital of Slovenia is Ljubljana?"

"Get him into line and get his chains off," the snatcher growled, jabbing a finger into Dom's chest. "Then keep him in line."

"Sure thing," Dom answered easily. "Wish I could offer you a mint."

The snatcher hesitated; eyes confused as he wondered how bad his breath must be if Dom had caught it, despite them both wearing masks.

Dom led Kiddo to the line, where now two others waited ahead of him.

Dom used his key to undo the chains connecting Kiddo's wrists and neck. He didn't have the key for the cuffs, because they were meant to stay on. But Kiddo wished he didn't have to feel so constricted – even wearing next to nothing else.

Maybe this was going to be the kind of fit where he gagged loudly. That could be theatrical.

His mind was slipping.

He blinked, and there was just one competitor ahead of him, now being walked out from the wings to the middle of the stage.

"You're ok," Dom was whispering.

He could tell Kiddo was losing it.

"Hang in there."

Kiddo shivered and shook out his arms as if he could get rid of the electricity running through them.

"I'm fine," he managed through gritted teeth. "This'll be good."

Then the lights turned red, and Dom was drawing Kiddo out to the middle of the stage.

"I won't be far," he promised, before melting away from Kiddo's vision, into the haze.

The judges, all of the Top Twos, madam and sir, were all close to the stage. Watching him expectantly. Hungrily.

But to Kiddo's staring eyes, their faces seemed to be merging into each other and then drawing apart.

He blinked. Swayed.

They waited with bated breath.

The music began first. Dramatic.

But the show really started when suddenly the lights switched to blackout mode.

There were gasps and rounds of applause as his body paint

made him into some kind of burning demon. He hadn't even moved yet.

Oh wait … his head was nodding rhythmically of its own accord, against his will.

The music was building.

Now his head was rolling on his shoulders. The burning, painted demon was possessed.

His arms were twitching. Like a zombie throwing its limbs forward to make them work.

The audience 'oohed'. As if this were quite the art-house performance.

And then the lights shattered everything in the world.

Moving, alternating beams projected over the stage.

High voltage. They bounced and flickered or shot straight out in laser rays.

They were everywhere. Blinding.

God, how it hurt.

Pierced him through the head like an arrow.

Where was he?

Why was this happening?

Surely the circuit-boards in this place would explode.

Definitely, Kiddo's circuits would.

The strobe lights took over, making his body alternate from lit up with paint to illuminated by flashes.

Kiddo screamed, writhed, collapsed, thrashed – legs kicking, screaming again, on repeat. Then laid still. Staring. Empty.

There were cheers.

They loved the spectacle. Thought it was a great show. Until he didn't get up and carry on entertaining them.

The lights turned to red again. The music kept pumping.

But there were arguing voices, and suddenly a monster – a snatcher mask was over Kiddo's line of sight. Madam and sir had found their way up onto the stage. The judges were circled around him, shouting in agitation over the music.

"He was so far ahead of the other tens," madam was screaming at the judges over the noise. "This doesn't even level the playing field!"

"Why haven't they turned the music off?" sir growled in annoyance, glaring toward the sound and light booth further back in the crowd. "I can see them scrambling around in there." He waved his arm erratically. "Turn it off!" he bellowed.

But the show went on, the music blasting. Because two Razes were starting to wreak havoc in the control booth – Jingle and Sparks were taking it over.

"For goodness' sake," madam shrieked at the judges, ironically – because she was not doing anything for the sake of goodness. "Stop putting crosses on his page!"

"I saw the Reykjaviks brushing up against this one before he went out on stage!" monster-snatcher-Dom declared accusingly. "They were working with the people from Juneau!"

"Reykjaviks?" sir yelled in consternation. "Juneau?"

"Capitals of Iceland and Alaska," Dom provided. "Did nobody listen to that poor girl's countries and capitals recital?"

"You see?!" madam announced, stabbing her finger in the air as if attacking it. "The other leaders have been trying to sabotage us!"

"How dare you?!"

"*You're* the ones with faulty security!"

"These attacks have been happening on *your* ground!"

"You've been making yourselves into the victims," someone else shouted. "Hoping the underdogs would win."

It turned out a whole host of reigning snatchers were up crowding the stage now. Ready to defend their already entirely tainted honour.

"Underdogs?!" sir spat incredulously. "Look at this competitor! The whole show should have been called off the minute we brought this one in!"

There were screams sounding over the music then, and the leaders turned about in confusion.

The buyers were screaming from the back rows, and on the sides of the room.

"Now what?" madam hissed with venom.

"Madam, sir," a snatcher raced through the crowd on the stage. "A bunch of the door and pod guards have been killed."

Razes, Razes, everywhere.

Snatchers, snatchers, all beware.

Kiddo smiled to himself. He was surfacing. Sluggish. But coming out of the phase.

"Some of the contestants have been unlocked and are loose!" the snatcher went on.

"They're *what*?!" the reigning snatchers started churning like a school of fish darting away from a dropped pebble. "This is going too far!"

Kiddo felt Dom grip him under the shoulders and start to drag him backwards along the stage floor before he could get stepped on by flustered leaders.

Crouching down, Dom pulled Kiddo to the backdrop of the stage, sitting Kiddo against himself so that he could wrap his arms around Kiddo protectively.

The red lights … were they pulsing?

More screams.

Snatchers, snatchers, all beware.

"Oh my God," someone said in a panic. "There are snatchers barring the doors down there, locking us in!"

Razes, Razes, everywhere.

Dom wrapped an arm around Kiddo's neck and half cradled his head, shielding Kiddo's eyes.

"It's about to get flashy and loud again, ok?" Dom said into his ear.

Kiddo nodded against Dom's protective hold.

He closed his eyes.

But he felt the blasts that followed to the tips of his hair, in the roots of his teeth, within the depths of his ear canals – which promptly popped.

He and Dom were pushed further backward and the backdrop rippled and swayed over them alarmingly.

Dom held him harder as more cracks sounded, and the whole exhibition hall seemed to rumble.

Was the whole concrete cavern going to collapse? Would the bay flood in?

Screams, shrieks and running feet were the tune playing between bangs and reverberations.

The fast swells of bright, fiery light were emanating through Kiddo's closed eyelids, and each one added a new layer of heat that sucked away his breath.

"Brace for the big one," Dom told him over the sound. "And pray Jingle worked out our chip immunity..."

Kiddo crushed himself against Dom, who held him tighter.

And then ...

A rippling wave.

Like a science demonstration of gravity.

A soundless, exploding bubble that burst over them, pushing against them, pushing in on them.

It sounded like they'd been plunged under water. Everything was thick and muted.

It felt like they were drowning. Weighed down.

Oh man.

Oh man ...

Kiddo needed to breathe, his lungs were straining.

And then it was washing over them and away.

They gaped like fish out of water.

Kiddo sagged against Dom, who sagged against the backdrop, which billowed in protest.

After a moment the music, which had still somehow kept playing, was cut.

The arena lights turned on.

The explosions were over.

And there were no more running feet.

"Competitors, please do not panic. You are being saved," Jingle's voice came over the speakers like that of some kind of omnipotent being. "Snatchers who fluked surviving, please panic. You are about to be found."

Kiddo gasped dizzily, the tension dropping from his body, and Dom moved his hand so that Kiddo could see.

An entire hall of snatchers and buyers. Razed to the ground.

| **30** |

Thirty

Hato was up on the stage almost immediately, mask off, sweeping in to hoist Kiddo up.

The side of Hato's face had a burn mark on it, and his hair was singed.

"I'm fine," Kiddo slurred.

Hato held Kiddo to himself even tighter.

"Dominic," Hato said in a very low voice – so low it sounded like he was talking around a throat lump bigger than his Adam's apple. "Thank you."

Dom tore his mask off at last with relief, and cast a hard eye around at the stage full of slumped, suited, gowned, jewelled, greedy bodies.

Bodies as far as the eye could see.

"Glad to help," he said darkly.

Hato gingerly picked his way over and around sprawled limbs, lowering Kiddo off the edge of the stage to Quicklips' waiting arms.

Quicklips beamed at Kiddo as if he really had been fearing

for his own brother's life, before he set him down in one of the judge's empty, throne-like seats.

One of Quicklips' teeth was missing, and he'd bled all over his snatcher outfit. But at least Kiddo didn't have to worry about salvaging that one in the wash.

Frazzle was there then, fussing over Kiddo, who was dimly staring about at the chaos – stupefied.

Dom was up on the stage, sitting on the chest of sir.

Sir, who was bleeding from the nose, mouth and ears, was floundering. Flapping his arms weakly.

Nobody else on the stage was moving.

As Kiddo watched, Dom slowly leaned forward.

Inch by inch, he pressed his hand and all of his weight behind it, against sir's throat.

Dom tilted his head, holding sir's gaze with his own, gradually leaning more heavily forward, until sir's arms stopped flapping.

Hato was beside Quicklips now, content that Kiddo was under Frazzle's care.

"Maybe we were a bit too keen with the explosives," Quicklips was saying, observing the crater-sized pockmarks in the cement walls. "It sure had the right effect though. And all the others will be perfect for tonight."

"We're going to have to be careful which exit we open in here," Hato grimaced. "This whole hall could collapse if we do something wrong."

"The support beams of this room are still intact," Quicklips reflected optimistically.

Seethe was roaming the arena, dealing with any snatchers who were still twitching. Probably too few for his liking.

Start was unlocking any shell-shocked, possibly still drug numbed competitors who hadn't yet been freed from their pods.

Trix had commandeered a mobile candy-bar trolley, and was handing out snacks and drinks to try to sober the competitors up.

Kiddo was surprised to see Velvet, consoling a younger contestant who was sobbing hysterically.

"Competitors, please do not rush for the exits. We are Raze. We are here to help you," Jingle was announcing, as if she'd been born to broadcast. "We will lead you out of this labyrinth all together. If you have no place to go, we will look after you."

"Oh, Kiddo …" Kiddo felt a familiar hand cup his cheek, and he turned to find Sparks.

"He's so hot," Sparks said to Frazzle, who nodded.

"Hey," Kiddo rasped at her. "You alright?"

She smiled, crouching down beside him. "I've just spent the last few hours helping to rig this whole underground city with explosives. I'm doing just fine."

She had a bruise across her cheek and a cut splitting the corner of her mouth. She and the others had obviously had some resistance to their coup.

Kiddo swallowed heavily – his mouth was so very dry.

"Too much drugs," Frazzle was telling Hato, Quicklips and now Dom. "He overheat and dehydrate. Pulse too high."

Dom swore. He looked ready to go back and suffocate sir again.

Sparks was pressing a bottle of water into Kiddo's hands

now, and she watched as it shook erratically while he raised it.

"Thanks," he said with some relief. "Where are ... Tiny and Flip?" he asked.

She took her now unneeded mask from her pocket, wetting it and starting to dab his skin down to cool him.

"Hey, keep your eyes open," she instructed.

"Mmm?"

"Flip and Tiny are driving snatcher vans through the society they've got ... they had ... going on out there," Sparks told him, wetting his hair and pushing it back so it drizzled in cool darts down his neck and shoulders. "It was honestly the most organised warren for a city below a city."

"They're ... joy riding through a ghost town?" Kiddo frowned.

"They're going to check every last bit of this place for any other prisoners who hadn't been sold and shipped, and will round them up," she answered. "When we know this place is clear, we're going to hit Jingle's remote detonator, and blow the whole thing up."

His pulse was throbbing in his temples. Was that normal?

"That'll be nice," Kiddo mumbled.

His chin hit his chest then. It was way too hard to hold such a heavy head up. Big ol head it was.

"Frazzle, is he alright?" Sparks cried out anxiously. "He's breathing really erratically."

"He need cool air," Frazzle's voice said. "He need home. Now."

"Trix and Start, hurry it up with the competitors!" Hato shouted. "Quicklips, work out which door is going to be safest and get us a clear exit." He raised his voice again then. "Jingle, radio for Flip and Tiny to come pick us up! We're going to need to make a lot of trips, but Kiddo is first out."

Dom's fingers were wrapped firmly around Kiddo's wrist now. An anchor.

And Sparks was wiping down his shoulders, cooling him as much as she could.

"My chest really hurts," Kiddo told Dom.

"Home," Frazzle repeated. "Now."

| 31 |

Thirty One

"He doesn't look so good."

Kiddo phased in with a pang when he heard Trix's voice, and felt himself being lowered into the back of the van.

He struggled, panicking.

He was being snatched!

"It's alright," Dom soothed. This time he didn't have a mask on. Kiddo could see the lotus on Dom's finger. He was holding Kiddo's hand, sitting on the hard floor of the van with him. "You're ok."

"Chuck us those peanuts from the candy-bar leftovers," Seethe was saying to Trix. "Frazzle wants to get some salt into Kiddo."

Trix threw a bag of peanuts to Frazzle, who was on Kiddo's other side. Seethe passed in more bottles of water.

But then Trix and Seethe were both out of the van. Sparks and the others were outside of the van too, far off in the distance. On the snatcher ramp. They were in the highway tunnel.

The rest of the van was cramped with strangers. All tens. Big eyes on him.

Kiddo fought to sit up again.

"Seethe! Trix! Sparks!" he yelled desperately. "Get in!"

Seethe and Trix turned back in surprise.

"Get in, *please!*" Kiddo almost sobbed. "They'll get you."

Seethe leaned back in the doorway of the van.

"Don't worry, Kiddo," he gave a murderer's grin. "There ain't no more snatchers left down here to snatch."

Dom was guiding Kiddo to lie back. Frazzle had the salt from peanuts all over his fingertips, and rubbed it across Kiddo's lips so they stung.

Kiddo couldn't help but lick his lips between gasps. Then gulped down the offered bottle of water appreciatively.

"Every Raze is going to grab a van and start driving competitors out of here," Trix told Kiddo then. "It'll be like when Dom led the horde of snatched kids out of the desert."

"We'll see you back at the warehouse," Seethe said. He helped one more ten into the van – a very regal Pash, still fully gowned, who accepted Seethe's assistance before Seethe closed the van doors.

There was the sound of two thumps from Seethe, and someone started the ignition, getting the van moving.

Kiddo's heart raced again.

"Oh my God, Dom," Kiddo cried, with tears streaking down the sides of his face. "They're going to get taken."

He tried to get up once more. Agitated.

"All of them," he said brokenheartedly.

Kiddo just could not get enough air.

He was gulping it in like a suffocating man.

Dom was trying to fan him down.

"Oh no," Frazzle said. "He going to seize again."

Kiddo hadn't even seen that one coming.

But he woke again to a prick in his arm.

There was the sound of running water, and he was ensconced in steam. But it was their own bathroom, back at the warehouse this time. And a bath was running.

Hato was carrying him toward the bath.

But he was already so hot.

"Where are they?" he asked hoarsely. "The others?"

Another pinch at his arm, in the crook of his elbow.

A drip was attached to him by a tube, which Dom was carrying alongside Hato, and Frazzle had given Kiddo a shot of something else.

"They're safe," Hato told him in his deep, calm voice. "Doing trips back and forth. On the surface at the docks, you can't tell yet that anything's happened. Nobody will be after them."

Kiddo squeezed his eyes shut with relief. Gulping down the emotion.

He'd been so convinced.

"I thought they were gone," he admitted shakily. "We lost them."

Hato lowered him into the warm water, and kept a hold under Kiddo's shoulders so he wouldn't slip all the way in.

Dom had Kiddo's drip bag lifted up, and also started to cup water over his chest at the same time.

Paint spread out from Kiddo like inky blood.

"How long until I don't just feel like one big heart beat?" Kiddo moaned.

Frazzle checked his watch, counting down before preparing another shot. "This the last dose. You calming down now."

Kiddo nodded his thanks and leaned his head back against Hato's chest. "Thought I was headed to a heart attack the way I was going."

"You was." Frazzle injected him a final time, unphased.

"I could kill them all again," Dom uttered sinisterly. "But there will be plenty of loose ends around the world that I can tie up."

Kiddo grabbed Dom's hand to stop it from pouring water over him. He dragged Dom's hand down to his heart, which truly was starting to feel less like a time bomb.

"Please don't talk about leaving just yet," he told Dom seriously.

And the tension left Dom's shoulders. "Course not," he soothed. "Hato's just given me a room and all," Dom's eyes flickered up to Hato's face beyond Kiddo's view. "So I'd never be gone long anyway. I don't want to be alone so much anymore."

When they helped him out of the water and he managed to get dry he was glad to peel the pointless shorts off and to find his own pyjama pants and bed.

He also didn't care how surprised they were – he hugged every single member of the team when they got in and Hato sent them up to see him.

They all showed signs of scuffles.

Flip was mourning the loss of his switch – which had been dropped somewhere. His hair was plastered to his face with blood and plaster powder, which he was on his way to wash off.

Tiny was limping.

Jingle had an icepack on her wrist.

Velvet had a badly broken nail, and patted him stiffly on the back.

Start was working out all the spare spaces in the whole warehouse to set up rest spots for rescued contestants.

Quicklips hadn't been able to find an after hours dental clinic, and was pretty sure his pearly-white tooth was dying in its cup of milk. But it didn't keep him from smiling and hugging Kiddo warmly in return.

All of them were battle weary. But all of them were alive.

Later when Trix and Seethe had found the right keys for undoing the candidates' cuffs, and when they came up to help Kiddo out of his, Seethe swore poisonously – but Kiddo was even happy to hear that level of normalcy from anyone in the gang.

"What?" Dom asked, hovering in concern.

Seethe swore again before he answered. He pointed at Kiddo's neck. "Look at that mark," he said with a filthy glare. "Absolute animals."

Dom hiccupped then, eyeing the love bite. "Oh. Yep. Those snatcher animals."

Sparks came up to lie on one side of Kiddo's bed, content to nap, and Dom sprawled out on the other side, lying on his stomach. He rested his chin in his hands and stared dreamily at Kiddo until Kiddo huffed in pretend annoyance and hit him with a pillow.

Kiddo's clock told him that it was somehow still Saturday evening.

He would think about his homework tomorrow.

For now, it was nice to be free. To be experiencing a Saturday night above ground. And nice to be right where he was.

| 32 |

Thirty Two

Kiddo rubbed his eyes. He was still in the jelly-bean shape his body had assumed around Sparks, though she must've slipped away.

"He's had more sleep than he usually does, and he'd hate to miss this," Dom's voice was insistent from outside Kiddo's doorway. "Of all of us, he should get to see this happen after the last few days."

"He needs to rest," Hato disagreed. "Frazzle is going to stay with him."

"Fine," Dom said. "But *I'll* stay."

"You'll stay?" Hato asked. "Of all people, you should also get to see this."

Kiddo could imagine Dom shrugging. "Tell Frazzle not to worry about the patient up here, he can focus on the other competitors you've got set up here. I'll take care of Kiddo."

"Alright," Hato answered slowly, trying not to sound suspicious of Dom. "We're taking the vans so they get wiped out too."

"Good choice. We don't need any links back to us," Dom agreed.

There was the sound of footsteps – Hato, and then presumably Dom taking hold of the handle.

"Hato …" Dom said, and the footsteps paused.

"Dominic?"

"We've done something incredible," Dom told him then. "We've turned the tides."

"We have," Hato replied sombrely. "And you coming home made all the difference."

Dom said nothing.

The footsteps resumed, moving down the stairway.

The door opened and Dom waited until Hato's weighted movements had faded out of earshot.

Then Dom peered at Kiddo and grinned.

"Ready to head out on an adventure?"

Kiddo snorted. He threw off his covers.

"Only if you're up for it," Dom said honestly. "You have to feel well enough."

"We'll go slow and use the library fire escape door, instead of the window," Kiddo told him.

"We have plenty of time," Dom assured him. "The gang need to clear the warehouses and cordon off the area so nobody randomly happens upon the docks even at this hour. They need to drop off the vans. And they need to double check it's just bodies down there."

Kiddo shuddered. He was glad he hadn't been considered to be up to such a grisly task. Even a chamber full of the bodies of those who deserved to be dead, was still a chamber full of bodies of dead people.

Dom chose some warm clothes for him and helped him pull them on.

They were quiet as they descended the outer stairs, blowing the smoke of the chilled air ahead of them.

"It's nice to walk the streets so late and not have to worry," Kiddo commented.

Dom kicked a pebble ahead of them so it skittered down the road. "Don't forget there are still random, horrible people out there," he reminded Kiddo brightly. "Just not part of large-scale, corrupt organisations."

"Hopefully our chances are better against a select few rotten apples though," Kiddo took his turn kicking the rock.

"Yes, especially when we just knocked off the worst of the bunch, which had been poisoning the most of the tree," Dom agreed. "With the rest of the buyers soon to follow by social crucifixion."

Kiddo blew more mist like smoke, nodding.

Dom walked backwards, like he had just the other day, and pulled Kiddo's collar up against the cold.

"Cover that hickey," Dom scolded, making Kiddo grin.

Kiddo kicked their rock again, and Dom fell back in at his side.

"What are you thinking?" Dom asked him then.

Kiddo thrust his hands into his pockets, but Dom freed one of his own hands from his leather jacket, and slid it into Kiddo's back jeans pocket.

"I'm thinking ..." Kiddo began with an effort. "That me asking you not to consider moving on again so soon was unfair."

Dom tugged Kiddo closer by his back pocket.

"Oh?" Dom questioned.

"It was selfish," Kiddo shrugged gloomily. "I know that now is the best time for you, and anyone else in the group who wants to continue on as Raze, to get out there and weed out snatcher leftovers in all kinds of places."

Dom sighed. "You're top of your classes for a reason."

Kiddo felt his still fragile heart sinking like a stone in water.

"It surprises everyone, every time," he said, eyes downcast.

"Not me," Dom answered. "And not really most people. Not the ones with eyes in their heads."

Kiddo pulled a face at him.

"Honest," Dom said stoutly. "There is a quiet brilliance about you, a constant current of energy, and also this need to stay under the radar that makes you one of the most interesting people in a room."

"You give me too much credit," Kiddo laughed, "you don't need to sweet-talk me like when we first met."

"Oh, I can smooze with the best of them," Dom stated. "But I always work with what I see as the truth."

Kiddo thought about it, and realised he'd noticed that in Dom. He said things straight.

"Thank you for thinking that," Kiddo told him.

They took their time, leisurely finding a good place in the fence by the docks, where it was easy enough to scale without having a literal heart attack.

"You shouldn't undersell yourself," Dom replied. "You're one of the cleverest, bravest, best people I've met. Especially when you get a little scrambled and jumpy," Dom smiled.

"Especially then?" Kid raised an eyebrow.

"Every person in the world has flustered moments. And there your brain is, trying to keep you in that state all the time. But look at you go. You run a household, you get through school, you take down empires."

"In the most hectic ways possible," Kiddo jibed.

"You do everything you can to still get the job done, and care very much when you can't. I'd say that points toward a worthwhile person."

Kiddo grimaced. "And you are the original Raze. You have the ability to find a way to dismantle every snatcher base around the world, before the leftover snatchers can get ideas of grandeur and regroup into a new reigning class."

"There are only one hundred and ninety-four of them now," Dom told him helpfully.

Kiddo winced. "Can you just do the top forty?"

Kiddo went first into their tunnel, and caught Dom before he toppled too far and shot out to the water.

Their tunnel appeared sturdy enough, being half sunken into dried mud, that it wouldn't roll off anywhere in the face of a mammoth blast on the other side of the docks.

"I'm not sure two minutes will cut it for my performance at each capital," Dom deliberated. "I could try."

They both sat facing toward the water, leaning shoulder to shoulder, with knees touching.

Dom didn't seem to mind that Kiddo was tapping a song on his thigh, and Kiddo didn't mind that Dom was absently rubbing his fingertips against the short sides of Kiddo's hair.

"Will you definitely come back?" Kiddo asked after a while.

"I'll be back for you by the time you're on the semester

break," Dom said with confidence. "And if the job's not done, I'll head back out after that."

"The job will never fully be done," Kiddo remarked. "It's impossible. It's not just tracking down offshoots of snatcher groups, which will spring up to test their new boundaries. It's all the kids who were like you, who you might be able to find."

"Ah," Dom rubbed the back of Kiddo's neck. "But if I've trained enough other Razes, me being there will hardly matter. And I'll be counting on the media to expose and liberate where needed too. So I'll come back as often as I can, even for short stays, just to remind myself I have a home."

Kiddo thought about it. "I suppose. Flip has done a similar thing for years."

"I think Flip and Velvet will be wanting to come," Dom said thoughtfully. "Maybe even Trix and Start."

"They will want something more, if there's less need to protect this area and The Lair now," Kiddo nodded. "They would come and go happily too. And Jingle would probably be happy to help you digitally from afar."

They quietened then, as they saw a flare rise up over the water.

That was the team's final warning to get clear of the snatcher side of the docks.

Everything must have been cleared, taped off and readied.

A moment later, there was the kind of light that an unseen bolt of lightning makes, as it flashes and seems to briefly illuminate the whole sky. But instead of silver, it was fiery amber. Instead of fading, it grew in intensity. And instead of thunder, there was a sound like an avalanche straight after.

Even the dark waters seemed to fill as if with magma from below the surface. Plumes of fire spurted from both sides of the pipes that concealed that awful ramp entrance. The warehouses covering an entire block – the snatcher underground, burst into fire from a blast that had shaken them from underneath, before they fell like burned out matchsticks.

The docks themselves creaked and rumbled, shifting and trembling, before suddenly the banks collapsed in on themselves. Everything was sinking inward, burning up, and then being extinguished dramatically by a flood of water that rushed on in to wash away the rot of what had been.

The quaking and groaning of the docks continued, and fires burned on. But at last they could see that what was left of this capital's snatcher empire was a deep, sunken-in, bite shaped chunk that had been taken out of the docks.

Kiddo watched the burning and the churning of the waters until Dom tugged at his hand and they pulled themselves away from their tunnel.

They had to beat Hato home. And had to be as far away from one of the biggest, most confusing crime scenes to have suddenly appeared out of nowhere.

"That was satisfying," Kiddo said at last, pulling his jacket tightly around himself. Now if he closed his eyes and had flashes of being snatched or tested or chained, he would fill his mind with those flames.

"Extremely," Dom agreed. "But … do you think you're all good, after what you went through?"

Kiddo shivered. "Nope. Not good. But I *will* be fine."

Dom looped an arm around Kid's neck.

"Now that was an honest answer," Dom said appreciatively. "Thank you."

"Another candid moment," Kiddo grimaced. "I hate the thought of sleep, of leaving school after detention, and of dinners without you there."

Dom grinned and pulled Kiddo in close so he could nuzzle into Kiddo's neck – right where the love bite already was.

That sent butterflies of memory skittering about in Kiddo's stomach.

"Well, a candid moment from me too, then," Dom drawled as they walked on. "Is that I swear, that no matter what's going on, I will definitely come back to you by the end of next year," Dom confided. "Because I hate how the other students at school look at you like they're a bunch of snatchers too."

"No they don't," Kiddo guffawed, but then lowered his voice to a whisper as they got to the warehouse fire escape. "I'm the mess who sits at the back."

Dom stopped him before he could open the library door, and pushed him against the stairwell, hands on either side of the rail so that Kiddo was looking him in the eye.

"A beautiful mess. Closest thing I ever saw to an eleven. And that's not a thing. You're turning heads while *your* head's ducked down."

Dom held his gaze for a second, then relented, and eased the door open to let Kiddo in.

They crept down as if Hato and every cop in the city were waiting for them, and stealthily slipped into Kiddo's room.

"Why did you decide that the end of next year is your definite deadline?" Kiddo asked curiously, hanging his jacket and turning to find Dom already stripped down and making himself comfortable in Kiddo's bed.

"Because Hato said you can't date 'til you finish school," Dom explained wickedly. "And in case you actually notice any of those other high-schoolers pining over you, I better make sure I'm back in town and ready."

"I see," Kiddo folded his shirt and trousers, then stretched out his stiff muscles with a wince.

Dom reached for him, and Kiddo obligingly sank into the bed beside him.

Dom didn't seem to mind Kiddo's elbow resting against his stomach, and Kiddo didn't mind Dom's hip against his.

"I won't be hurt if Sparks is the first person you properly make love to across that time apart," Dom announced after a bit. "But if that happens, I want to be second," he said resolutely. "After that, fine fine, we're not conventional."

Kiddo smiled despite himself.

"Dom?"

"Yeah?"

"No fear."

There was a pause.

"… None?"

"Sparks was right the other day. You're one of the best things to have happened to us," Kiddo said. "Because of you, things have happened for me. Because of you, I've also survived other things that have happened *to* me. Even with you gone, I think I'll do better at trying to remember to sleep."

"You'll get someone else to pinch your neck?"

"No," Kid laughed. "Because I'll be shutting my eyes knowing that things seem more right in my world."

"Oh," Dom said, his voice touched. "Then no fear."

"None."

| 33 |

Thirty Three

"Ten minutes late this time," the teacher tutted, but then faltered at the thousand-watt beam of a smile that Kiddo gave as he slouched down at his desk.

"I'm just glad to have made it, ma'am."

What a relief to worry about things like his shirt being inside out and his tie being crumpled – because of course, nobody else had done the washing after Thursday night.

He held up his homework as the teacher came around, ready for collection.

"I like your new haircut," a couple of students whispered across the row, and he nodded his thanks, rubbing his hand over the back of his head.

The two students blushed when he gave some of his thousand-watt beam to them too.

"You noticed people noticing you for once, didn't you?" Dom moaned as he slipped down from the pillar and slung Kiddo's bag over his shoulder.

"I always felt like they were staring at my sloppiness and things I'd messed up," Kiddo admitted. "But today, even having the ability to be a relatively normal person in school was amazing."

"I get it," Dom said. "Normal is nice."

"You could come back after next year and do some normal with me, and with Sparks," Kiddo consoled him.

"Bet on it," Dom promised with feeling.

He helped Kiddo sear the beef and make the cheese sauce for the vegetables.

And Kiddo smiled when he noticed Velvet come up to set out the napkins, Quicklips get up from the couch to put out the cups, Sparks pour the drinks, Start set out the cutlery, and Flip yelling out to the others that dinner was going to be served so they should hurry up.

They were providing for even more people now. Anybody who had stuck around after being rescued too.

Future Razes.

During dinner, Start laid out a fresh collection of laminated maps. He'd already begun circling where he thought the most activity in each capital of the world had been, and where there might be groups of buyers still hoarding their stock and slave driving them.

Quicklips had left the TV on in the lounge area, and the news was delivering a report on recent shock arrests of the rich and famous. There was surprise over how many big names on the mysterious dark web list could not be found – they seemed to have just disappeared. But rather than the story being a disillusioning tale of apparently wonderful elites falling from grace, the story was about the public's growing vigilance, and a desire for revolution of the system.

Sparks was full now, and had her hand on his bouncing knee.

Dom was leaned back in his chair, blue eyes keen on the maps as he mulled over starting points with Flip. His arm was over the back of Kiddo's chair, and he was rubbing absently at Kiddo's shoulder to work out a kink in the muscle.

Kiddo knew he would be back.

It would feel like Kiddo had lost a piece of himself.

But that piece would come back.

| 34 |

Thirty Four: Epilogue

Kiddo started awake, his senses telling him he must.

He sat up, his eyes darting to the window.

It was ajar.

He had not left it that way. Had he?

"What's wrong?"

Kiddo turned slowly to where the side of his bed was weighted down a little by Sparks. She snuggled in closer to him, not really awake.

"Nothing. It's alright," he said with a frown, reaching to stroke her hair and to pull the covers up over her shoulders.

She was already breathing like a dreamer once more. And Kiddo's heart was settling to a normal rhythm again.

"You made stroganoff for dinner," a grateful whisper came from the door as it was opened a sliver, a figure entered, and then it was closed. "I needed that."

Quicklips was going to be devastated that the leftovers were gone, but Kiddo was gaping at Dom.

Dom flashed him the most impish grin to have ever been flashed.

He knelt down on Sparks' side of the bed, and pulled the cover that Kiddo had just lifted, back down again so that he could drink her in. Then he planted a deep kiss on her lips, trailed lighter kisses on her collarbones, and pressed one kiss to the skin of her stomach, exposed below the hem of her singlet and above her underwear line, for good measure.

She giggled drowsily, and shifted a bit as he tucked her back up.

Then he rounded on Kiddo, stripping as he circled the bed.

"Dom?" Kiddo managed at last.

"In the flesh," Dom agreed, and with one deft move, his cold, bare chest was getting some skin-on-skin action with Kiddo's. "Didn't you expect me?"

"Well," Kiddo answered, closing his eyes at the feel of Dom's hand trailing over his core. "It has only been a month. I don't have holidays for a few weeks yet."

Dom rested his arm over Kiddo in a way that was so right.

"Huh," Dom whispered next to his ear. "Only a month. It sure sucked though, didn't it?"

"It sure sucked." Kiddo agreed.

"Flip and I came back to see if Hato might start up a mentor program for all these lost kids we're finding." Dom said then. "Which would mean I'd be escorting them regularly."

"There will always be room for you."

"Hopefully my bed will be loaned out, and so there'll have to be room for me here, with you."

Dom bit into Kiddo's shoulder lightly. Cheekily.

"There will *always* be room for you, right here, with me."

RECEIVE YOUR EXTRA RAZE WARFARE CHAPTER WHEN YOU SIGN UP FOR SHELLEY CASS' VIP LIST. GET YOUR BONUS HERE:

shelleycass.com/coming-soon-02

OTHER BOOKS BY SHELLEY CASS

The Raze Warfare Series
'A Fairy's Tale' Epic Fantasy Series:
Book One – 'The Last Larnaeradee'
Book Two – 'The Raiden'
Book Three – 'The Army for the World'
Dystopian Future:
'Awaken Dreamer'
Contemporary/Action/Fantasy/Erotica:
'Darkling'
The Sleep Sweet Series for children:
Book One – 'Little Pixie's Christmas'
Book Two – 'The case of the bored baby Ace'
Book Three – 'Mum and Me'
Book Four – 'The Cloud and the Flower'
Book Five – 'Hush'

Dear reader,
I would love to hear your feedback!
Please leave a review and feel free to visit my author Facebook page
or website (shelleycass.com).

ABOUT THE AUTHOR

I was an awkward, reserved year 8 student – totally in love with the escape offered by the novels I read. I could hear the voices of the authors' characters, I could tune out my stresses and uncertainties as I journeyed with each protagonist through their own troubles. And then one day I could hear the voices of characters who hadn't been written yet, in places that hadn't been created, and I decided to write my own worlds.

In the real world I became a high school teacher, and still face the epic battle of staying afloat in all the papers I must assess. And in the real world the magic has also sometimes been hard to find. Stress and disunity surface like cancer – making the nightly news too hard to watch.

But in the real world there has also been inspiration – incredible students, loved ones, golden memories, growing up, warm hugs, big laughs and good people.

One of the greatest things achieved in my lifetime that I can remember, and that had a profound impact on me, was when Australia legalised equal marriage. I'd had this terrible sick fear that it wouldn't happen, and that I would have to face the fact that a majority of the people in my country do not want progress or equality. I would have to face the fact that some of my students and friends would not have the same rights or access to a future that I could choose to have. Teaching teens to reach for their dreams in a climate like that just seemed too hopeless. But instead, I remember sitting next to mum – happy tears streaming down her face – as something incredibly good was achieved. We proved that the majority of people appreciate love and the right to love in all forms. That love is love. Which is damn important in a world that can be so harsh.

So I wrote of the things that threaten the world, and of the big and small things that save it. I wish for a real world where the air is clean, the trees can grow without concrete borders, the darkness can be cured with the switch of a light, and the people can all have long days and happy lives.

ACKNOWLEDGMENTS

I am so thankful for the friends who understand me and embrace who I am.

I am so appreciative of my work family, for being my silver lining even on the most stressful days.

I am so appreciative of Wendy – the greatest neighbour to have ever lived, and Linda – the greatest mother to have ever lived. Your patience with reading my novels when they are still rough, clunky, colossal things is indescribably helpful.

I am so grateful for an extended family of extensive love: the bubbly and boisterous Brittinghams, Burkes and Rigbys, and the gracious, gorgeous Tangees, Lennens and Plants. My grandparents too, though lost, are such a special part of me.

I am so thankful for Linda (mum) and Robert (dad), who would move heaven and earth to make us happy.

For my sisters and best friends, Melissa and Leigh.

For my brother in law, Andrew, and the lights of my life – Jack and Elyssia.

For the love of my life, my sunshine, Jarryd.

And for the little year eight version of me, who first picked up that pen to write.